MR FAIRCLOUGH'S INHERITED BRIDE

Georgie Lee

MILLS & BOON

First Published in Great Britain 2019
by Mills & Boon, an imprint of HarperCollins*Publishers*
1 London Bridge Street, London, SE1 9GF

© 2019 Harlequin Books S.A.

Special thanks and acknowledgement are given to Georgie Lee
for her contribution to the Secrets of a Victorian Household series.

ISBN: 978-0-263-27280-2

MIX
Paper from
responsible sources
FSC™ C007454

This book is produced from independently certified FSC™ paper
to ensure responsible forest management.
For more information visit www.harpercollins.co.uk/green.

Printed and bound in Spain
by CPI, Barcelona

A lifelong history buff, **Georgie Lee** hasn't given up hope that she will one day inherit a title and a manor house. Until then she fulfils her dreams of lords, ladies and a Season in London through her stories. When not writing she can be found reading non-fiction history or watching any film with a costume and an accent. Please visit georgie-lee.com to learn more about Georgie and her books.

To Anne, always in our hearts.

To Grandma, thank you.

Chapter One

Baltimore—September 1842

'Gentlemen, listen.' Silas rapped his knuckles on the polished top of the rosewood dining table, bringing the boisterous men in their black dinner jackets and white waistcoats surrounding it to attention. 'If we can manufacture iron rails in America instead of relying on England, we could dominate the competition.'

'But the English rails are far superior to ours,' Mr Penniman answered, resting his hands on his round stomach. 'As are their engines.'

'They're cheaper, too,' Mr Baxter added, flicking away a small crumb sitting beside his plate.

'The prices will shoot up if the government changes the tariff rates or something interrupts the English supply,' Silas reminded them, determined to win these investors over to his idea. 'If we build our own foundries and hire the best iron workers, buy from the best domestic suppliers, we can produce our own rails and lay them ten times quicker than the competition. It'll ensure that the Baltimore Southern Railroad is the most impressive in America and at the forefront of innovation and development. We could even manufacture our own locomotives.'

The table erupted in a cacophony of disbelief and amazement with Mr Penniman and Mr Baxter astounded by the idea while Mr Wilson and Mr Farrow marvelled at the possibility.

At the far end of the table, Richard Jackson, Silas's business partner and mentor, remained silent where he sat beside Lady Mary Weddell, his ward and hostess for tonight. He allowed the men to argue among themselves and left it to Silas to convince the wealthy investors to part with more money than they'd already supplied to the Baltimore Southern. Silas would not disappoint Richard or himself or allow other men's lack of vision to dry up his income and keep him from sending home the money his family relied on for their up-keep. The Baltimore Southern would grow and succeed. He'd make damn sure of it.

'America is heading west, gentleman.' Silas raised his voice to gather the men's attention. 'When her boundaries reach the Pacific Ocean, new ports and trade routes with South America and the east will open up and provide untold opportunities. The railroads will be key to bridging the continent and reaping the benefits of those new opportunities.'

'You can't imagine the railways will stretch that far?' Mr Penniman leaned forward to see past the other men to Silas. 'It would take an engineering feat of immense proportions to traverse the Sierra Nevada.'

'In time we'll have those engineers and the equipment capable of conquering mountains. Already we've made it so that a man travelling from Kentucky to Washington, D.C. can do it in four days by rail instead of three weeks on horseback. Imagine being able to cross the county in a matter of weeks, of goods and raw materials reaching factories and markets as quickly. With your investment in the foundry we can take the first steps towards claiming this magnificent future.'

The men nodded and mumbled their agreement. Even those who'd been hesitant tilted their heads in thought at Silas's proposal. Silas shifted in his chair, determined not to betray the excitement surging inside him. He'd won them over. He could feel it.

'You do dream big, Mr Fairclough,' the balding Mr Penniman said before leaning over to take the last sweet from the platter in the centre of the table.

'His big dreams will overshadow all of us one of these days,' Richard added, finally making his presence as the senior partner and the owner of this house felt. He held a handkerchief to his mouth and coughed as quietly as he could before sliding it back into his pocket. 'The smart man would buy into the future while it's still affordable.'

'I assure you, gentleman, we aren't the only ones having this discussion, but we must be the first to put our plans into action.' Silas motioned for his valet, Tibbs, to instruct the footmen silently waiting along the periphery of the dining room to refill the brandy glasses with the fine vintage Silas had procured from one of his best English sources. None of the servers made a move to top up Silas's glass, though. Tonight required a clear head.

Mr Penniman covered the top of his crystal glass with his hand, glancing at Lady Mary Weddell to say that it was in deference to her that he exercised restraint. 'No, thank you, I think I've had enough for the evening.'

'Don't deny yourself the pleasures of Mr Fairclough and Mr Jackson's generosity on my account, Mr Penniman,' Lady Mary encouraged, offering him and a number of the other gentlemen a smile that saw them sit back and allow their glasses to be refilled. 'I refuse to let my presence parch a gentleman, especially while discussing matters that require a robust thirst.'

She motioned for a footman to place a new tray of sweets on the table in front of Mr Penniman. She'd been so sly in her ordering of the extra treats that not even Silas had noticed their arrival in the dining room. *Clever girl.*

Mr Penniman didn't hesitate to select the largest chocolate dusted with white sugar.

'You're a very smart woman, Lady Mary. You'll make some man very lucky one day.'

Lady Mary's smile remained as beguiling as before but the sparkle she'd turned on Mr Penniman dulled. He was oblivious to the change in her as he savoured the chocolate, but Silas noticed it. It was the same painful regret that used to mar the drawn faces of the women who regularly appeared on the doorstep of the Fairclough Foundation, begging for help. He doubted Lady Mary shared that sort of misery, but the nagging feeling that something unpleasant had brought her to America was as difficult to ignore as her help in wooing the investors.

Silas motioned for Tibbs, who leaned down beside him. 'Send Lady Mary a nice gift, something to thank her for her assistance tonight.'

'How nice a gift, sir?' The mental tally of Tibbs's contacts at various Baltimore shops and goldsmiths was almost visible in his light grey eyes.

'Ladylike exquisite.' Silas raised his half-drunk glass of brandy to Lady Mary, who nodded serenely. She was a plain young woman he guessed to be about three or four years younger than his twenty-five, with lively and intelligent brown eyes which seemed to miss nothing about her surroundings. She wore her blonde hair in a more mature fashion without the barrel curls most young women preferred. Her slender waist and stomach were accentuated by full breasts that were well hidden beneath a high-necked and far too plain dark grey gown. Despite the puritan simplicity of her attire, she sat with the poise of a queen, seeing over the table and the dinner arrangements with the panache of an experienced hostess. If she wore better dresses and did her hair in a more becoming fashion, she would be striking, but standing out, as Silas had learned during the three months that she'd lived with Richard, was not her habit. Instead, she remained discreetly present, understanding the gravity of what Richard and Silas were trying to accomplish and coyly doing all she could to help them achieve it.

'Yes, sir.' Tibbs straightened and Silas was certain Lady Mary would like whatever Tibbs selected for her. Silas couldn't speak to her tastes for he'd never enjoyed a private conversation with her beyond the weather. Despite them both being from England, she didn't hail from the same barely respectable part of London that Silas did. Thankfully, most Yanks didn't recognise the subtle difference in their accents, all to Silas's benefit. The higher up the social ladder they believed him to be, the more favourably they viewed him and his *wild* ideas.

'Gentlemen, here's to us and the future success of the Baltimore Southern's expansion.' Richard raised his brandy glass, the level of the liquid inside of it as unchanged as Silas's glass. The guests raised their drinks in answer, offering up a supportive cheer that made Silas smile. They'd secured the investors, even Mr Penniman who smiled at Lady Mary as widely as he did whenever his horse placed first in a race. Silas drained his brandy and motioned for Tibbs to refill it, ready to celebrate before tomorrow and the hard work began.

'We did it.' Silas relaxed into the leather wing-backed chair in Richard's study and stretched his feet towards the roaring fire in the grate. The study was an impressive room full of fine wood furniture and leather chairs where Richard had spent years building up his wealth through various business ventures, though it was the railroads that were closest to his heart, as they were to Silas's. Silas had been speechless the first time he'd stood in here, having stepped off the boat from England the day before, and he'd promised himself that one day he'd have a room like this. It was a pleasure to sit in this chair tonight and think of his study at home and how he'd achieved almost every goal he'd set for himself since leaving Liverpool nearly five years ago.

'Not we, you.' Richard removed his handkerchief from his pocket and coughed into it.

'They wouldn't have supported me if it weren't for your influence.' Silas traced the bottom of his brandy glass, wishing his ideas could stand on his reputation and merit, but he had yet to cultivate that kind of influence. More years in Baltimore establishing roots and a string of successes as long as the Baltimore Southern's tracks would earn him the respect he craved. Until then, he was thankful for Richard's influence and every opportunity he'd provided Silas since Silas had arrived in America.

Without Richard, Silas would still be the penniless, prospectless nobody he'd been when he'd left Liverpool. Silas tapped his glass with the pad of his finger. He'd never be that man again. 'I've already applied to the English patent owner for permission to build his locomotive here. Given what we've already invested in the steam works, it needs to start producing engines as soon as possible.'

The rails manufactured in the new foundry could be sold to other railroads to offset the cost of the Baltimore Southern's investment, but stronger, faster engines were the real key to railroad's future. Silas wished there were better American models to be had, but his adopted country had yet to produce a winning design. In time he was sure they would, but at present he needed the rights to the British one.

'That engine will take the Baltimore Southern to new heights and success.' Richard inhaled, the air rattling through his chest. 'But sooner than any of us would like, you'll have to win over investors without me.'

'You aren't thinking of retiring, are you?' Richard lived for his work.

'I'm dying, Silas.'

The same tightening of his stomach that'd almost made him retch ten years ago when his mother had stepped out of his father's sickroom to hand Silas his father's signet ring hovered about him like the heat from the fire. 'What are you talking about?'

'I consulted a number of medical men while I was in Philadelphia, the best in the country. They confirmed what I've suspect for some time.'

'That can't be.' Silas hadn't missed the coughing or the gradual thinning of Richard's body over the last year, but he'd ignored it and everything it meant, hoping it wasn't true, willing it to not be true. 'There must be some treatment here or in Europe. They're more advanced there than most of the quacks here who still think bleeding is the cure for everything.'

'No, Silas, you and I can struggle and strive against a great many things, but not this.' Richard sank into his chair, his slender body almost engulfed by the rich leather. 'I only regret that I won't be able to see the transcontinental railroad you envision. You're a dreamer, with a knack for making them come true, and I'm proud of you for it and for everything you've done since you first showed up on my doorstep with a letter of introduction from Jasper King and little more than a worn suit and a couple of British pounds. I took a chance that you were worthy of Jasper's trust and mine, and you've proven me right at every turn. You've gone from someone with nothing to part-owner of a railroad with a tidy income of your own that will only grow a great deal larger after tonight.'

'Don't curse us. All we have are their promises. We don't have their money yet or the tracks laid or the patent to the English steam engine.' Silas took a deep pull of brandy. Apparently, they didn't have a future together in the venture either. No, many people lived with consumption for years, there was no reason to think Richard couldn't, too.

'I don't mean the railroad. I have no children, no wife, my life spent married to my business and increasing my fortune. There are days when I think that was a mistake, until I see you.' He reached over and laid a fatherly hand on Silas's arm. 'You're like a son to me,

Silas, I don't want to see the same loneliness befall you.'

'It won't. In time, I'll marry.' Matrimony was not uppermost in his mind tonight, or any other night as of late.

'I also don't want to have what I've built up fall to pieces. I'm leaving you not only my share of the railway, but almost all of my estate.'

'I don't want it.'

Or deserve it.

He didn't wish to make his fortune by inheriting it from his mentor.

'I still insist you have it, at least everything I'm not leaving to Lady Mary. She'll get the house and a tidy financial settlement. It would mean the world to me if you'd look after her when I'm gone. She may not be related to me by blood, but she did a great deal for my sister in her last years and she's brought me immense comfort over these past three months. I want to leave her with a secure future so she never has to want or worry about anything.'

'Of course I'll make sure she and her investments are well protected.' Silas watched the flames in the grate leap and fall as they consumed the log. He understood the importance of protecting those he cared about. The cheques he regularly sent home to England supported his mother and sisters so that the donations to the Fairclough Foundation could continue to help the women in need. He threw back the rest of the brandy, the sting to his throat making his eyes water. Yes, he took care of his family with money, but little else. What else could they expect of him? He'd never wanted to be part of the Foundation, and if he hadn't come here to work with Richard there wouldn't be money to send home. It was the same circular thinking that plagued him every time he thought about how far away he was from his loved ones. He refilled his empty glass. Tonight, he had no patience for those old regrets.

'But of course, money isn't everything,' Richard mused.

'No, it isn't.' Silas set his drink on the table, all too familiar with that tone. The promise of a business proposal crackled in the air like the sap from the logs in the fire. What the devil could his friend be about to propose at a time like this?

'There are other, less tangible things to consider, such as standing, influence, a gentleman giving off the right sort of air when negotiating business or society, as you witnessed tonight.'

'I don't exactly smell of the fish market.'

'But you need that little something extra to raise everyone's opinion of you even higher.'

'Is it that low?' Silas laughed. He occasionally enjoyed a good game of cards at the clubs or a few other carnal pleasures when the need arose, but he'd never been in debt, got drunk or landed a woman, respectable or not, in any difficulty. He'd seen what'd happened to those unfortunate women enough times growing up at the Fairclough Foundation to ensure no woman suffered because of his attention or her situation in life. 'Given the way the mothers throw their daughters at me at the balls, I thought I was rather admired by Baltimore society.'

'In every endeavour there is always room for improvement.' Richard opened the small humidor on the table beside him and held it out to Silas. Silas selected a cigar from the box. He didn't smoke often, but something in Richard's manner told him this occasion called for it or a stiffer drink. Richard took a cigar from the humidor and set the box back on the table. He withdrew the silver clipper on the chain from his waistcoat pocket, snipped off the end and set it between his lips. He leaned forward, accepting a light from Silas who held out a small stick from the fire. Richard inhaled deeply as he sat back before taking the cigar out of his mouth and exhaling with a wincing cough that saddened Silas. 'You need the kind of improved opinion that an impressive and respectable marriage confers on a man.'

Silas choked on the smoke and the unexpected suggestion. 'The kind of respectability you never sought for yourself.'

'I almost did once, many years ago when I lived in Mobile. I was in the cotton business back then and on my way to making my first real fortune. We were in love, but yellow fever stole her from me. I never found another like her after that.'

It was the first time Silas had ever heard Richard speak with such affection about a woman who wasn't his now-departed sister in England. It tightened his chest to realise Richard might be reunited with both women far too soon. 'Then what's turned your thoughts to matrimony?'

'Your future and Lady Mary's.' He wheezed as he exhaled smoke. 'A well-settled woman isn't a single one at the mercy of every fortune hunter in the States, but a married one with a home and family, one who can successfully host dinners and help further your interests because they are her own.'

Silas took a deep drag off the cigar. He'd never in all their time together ever questioned Richard's reasoning for anything. He hated to make an exception this far into the game. 'I give you my word that I'll make sure she's well protected from fortune hunters and that she contracts a good marriage.'

Richard threw back his head and laughed, the cheerful sound weighted down by the rattle marring it. 'Shame on me for not being more direct.'

'You're being very direct.' A little bit too much for Silas's liking. He'd always imagined himself settling down some day, but not quite this soon and not with a near stranger. Lady Mary was a pleasant enough woman, but he knew almost nothing about her. He wasn't one to pry into other people's affairs, at least those not connected to business that could benefit him in negotiations. 'But the lady and I aren't well acquainted.'

'Not a difficult problem to rectify.'

'She may not be amenable to the idea.'

'Again, not an insurmountable obstacle.' Richard leaned towards Silas, the firelight highlighted the growing gauntness in his face. Richard was very sick, there was no denying it or what it meant. Once again Silas would be left alone in the world to make his way through it. He might not be the fifteen-year-old boy who'd taken on the responsibilities of a man far too soon, but it was difficult to hold that old apprehension at bay. 'This isn't merely a matter of the heart, Silas, but a very practical union that could benefit you both. I know I haven't told you a great deal about Lady Mary so I'll tell you what I can. She's the Earl of Ashford's daughter.'

That was nothing to scoff at and plenty of reasons to wonder. 'Then what's she doing here? Why isn't she in London where her mother can marry her off?'

Richard rolled his cigar between his fingers. 'That's something you'll have to hear from the lady herself.'

Silas was certain he didn't need to ask. There was only one reason a man as high up the social scale as an earl would cast out a daughter. Silas had never met any woman so high, but he'd met plenty of other young women from good families at the Foundation. The details were different, but the story was always the same—a man, a lapse of judgement and a very distinct alteration of their future, fortunes and standing. Silas had never held it against them. His parents hadn't raised him with such prejudices. Besides, having made more than a few of his own mistakes, he could understand theirs and that the men were as much to blame as the women for what had happened. 'But what's the benefit of her over, say, Mr Penniman's daughter?'

'One—' Richard held up a single finger '—never mix business with pleasure. Better to keep someone like Mr Penniman as an investor rather than a father-in-law. He'll have less say in your affairs and it won't be awkward if things turn sour. Two—' he held up another finger '—her standing as a genuine lady. Americans already think any man who sounds like you is an aristocrat. If you have a wife on your arm and at the head of your table who actually is one, it'll raise you even higher in their esteem. America is full of younger sons of the nobility trying to make a fortune, but an available young woman with Lady Mary's lineage is a rare find. The two of you could really make something of yourselves.'

'We'd make another commoner, like me, the son of an earl's fourth son who preferred humanitarianism to hunting. I've never even met the Lord my grandfather, who probably doesn't know I exist.' A fact his father and mother's passion for philanthropy had reminded him of daily while he was growing up. Silas took a sip of the fine brandy, savouring the sharp flavour. Bless his parents for their altruism. It wasn't the way he wished to live.

'But you know he exists. I've heard you drop his name during more than one conversation when it's to your benefit to do so.'

Silas shrugged. 'A man uses what slender means he has available and I assure you mine are very slender.'

'With Lady Mary by your side your means will widen considerably. You could affix her family crest to your carriage or have a combination of hers and yours created. Imagine how that would look at the top of your letter head or on calling cards. You could even incorporate it into the Baltimore Southern's insignia, give the railway a touch of English class to really impress merchants and passengers,' Richard suggested, the way he did whenever he thought aloud about how to approach investors for a new venture. It was the idea one had to sell, not the business. Never that. It was too ordinary and boring for a man to really picture, but an idea, slightly exaggerated in its aspects but never lied about, something an investor could hold in his mind when he held the stock certificate, that was something else. It was Richard's gift, one that Silas had worked hard to cultivate over the last five years. He never imagined it being used on him to propose a match as if Richard were some kind of hovering mother at a ball.

Silas took another drag off his cigar, turning the smoke into rings as he carefully exhaled. 'Even if I was for it, what would the lord and lady think of this match?'

'They gave up the right to approve or disapprove of her decisions some time ago,' Richard spat, then took a calming puff off his cigar. 'Besides, they aren't here to look down their regal noses at you, now are they? Nor are they likely to leave their hallowed estate and venture across the Atlantic to make a stink about it.'

'No, they aren't.' Silas inhaled the weedy smoke of his cigar while he thought over Richard's proposal as he'd considered every other business decision Richard had ever placed in front of him. Silas wasn't ready to invest in Lady Mary yet but the benefits of the match, like those of a foundry for the Baltimore Southern, were compelling enough to be considered.

An interesting idea, Mary mused silently while she stood in the shadows outside the study, listening to the men. This wasn't the first time she'd hovered out of sight in the darkness while others discussed her future. It was becoming quite the regular habit where her life was concerned. At least this time the proposed plan was kindly meant and to her benefit because Richard genuinely cared about her. It was more than her parents could ever have said about their actions. Their love of reputation and standing had been more valuable to them than their daughter.

She touched the small watch hanging from a ribbon on her dress bodice, a gift from Ruth, Richard's sister, during Mary's first Christmas with her. She ran her fingers over the fine filigree, feeling the few strands of the fraying ribbon on which it hung. The watch was one of the many kindnesses Ruth had shown her during the years that Mary had spent with her. She missed Ruth, but she was ashamed to say she didn't miss the isolation of the country.

Quiet spread over the room, broken by the pop and crackle of the fire and Richard's occasional cough, one that cut through Mary as sharply as his sister's final illness had. Richard knew Mary's secret and, like his sister, he'd given her a chance to reclaim some of the life and future that Preston Graham had stolen from her. It was everything she'd sought when she'd staggered off the ship still green with seasickness and breathed in the salty Baltimore air tinged with smoke. All the training to be a lady and chatelaine of a large house that her mother had drilled into her as a child—how to host a table, draw up menus, guide conversation, the skills she should have used as the wife of a titled man—was finally being put to use in Richard's house. She'd been awkward and reserved, hesitant and unsure when Richard had initially encouraged her to meet with the housekeeper about dinner or sit at the head of his table. Tonight, it'd all come back to her as the food had been well received and served, and the conversation had run smooth enough to ease Richard and Mr Fairclough's negotiations. She'd left the dining room with a new confidence and for the first time in many years the belief that her future would finally shake free of her past.

Death was threatening to steal it away from her for the second time. What would she do without Richard to guide her through Baltimore society? She'd be left on her own once again to make her way in a world that was even more foreign to her than the wilds of Devon and an aged spinster's humble but welcoming cottage.

Mr Fairclough's deep voice, his accent a touch less refined than her father and brother's, but far from the roughness of the London streets or fields, cut through the quiet with some matter of business. The tone of his voice held her interest, the notes of it deep and sure the way Preston's had been during those darks nights in the stable or his carriage, until it'd turned callous and cold like the road to Gretna Green.

Mary slipped away from the door and through the narrow entrance hall of the brick row house with its marble floors and tall ceilings, and up the polished wood staircase to her room. She sat at her dressing table, leaving the bell to summon Mrs Parker, her lady's maid, untouched. Despite having grown up with a nurse to feed and care for her, a governess to teach her and, when she'd finally come out in society, a lady's maid to see to her beautiful ball gowns and carriage dresses, the last four years of attending to herself made her hesitant to ring the bell.

No, not any more.

She was no longer a companion but a lady and she would never be anything less ever again. She picked up the bell and shook it, the tinny noise cutting through the still of the room.

'You're upstairs early tonight, Lady Mary.'

Mrs Parker beamed as she came in from the adjacent room. Mary smiled at the older woman's American frankness. If a lady's maid had ever addressed her mother in so informal a manner she would have been dismissed without a reference. That strict distance between servants and employers had seemed so right and proper to Mary back then. It didn't any more.

'It was a successful, if not tiring one.' It'd taken a great deal of organising prior to the dinner to make everything during it seem effortless and serene, and Mary was eager to sleep. She would need all the rest she could gather to get through the difficulties she was sure to face in the coming months if Richard's health declined as quickly as his sister's had. She'd seen the bloody handkerchiefs and heard the rattle in his chest, the same one that had claimed Ruth in the end. Mary clutched the watch on the ribbon, her eyes misting with tears. She was tired of losing people she cared about and who genuinely cared about her.

'There, there, Lady Mary, what's the matter?' Mrs Parker laid a comforting hand on Mary's shoulder and she didn't shrug it off

the way her mother had when her old house-
keeper had tried to comfort her after the death
of Mary's grandmother. Instead, Mary welcomed the kind gesture. It reminded her of
Ruth.

'Nothing, only I'm a little tired from tonight's excitement.' There was no point ruining her evening, too. She would learn the
truth about Richard soon enough assuming she
didn't already know.

Mrs Parker nodded her head, making the
pile of grey hair arranged in a careful twist
on top of it shiver with the motion. 'I'll get to
laying out your nightclothes and have the maid
send up the water to wash your face.'

'Thank you, Mrs Parker.'

'My pleasure.' She turned and began to bus-
tle about, removing Mary's fine linen nightgown from the dresser, the one she'd purchased
to replace the plain cotton ones she'd arrived
with, and laid it out on the coverlet. 'It's so
nice to have a young person in the house and
a lady's touch to soften things about the edges,
but if you don't mind my saying, some places,
like this room, could do with a little more feminine charm.'

'Yes, it could.' Mary hadn't made any changes to the room since she'd been here, leaving the handsome furniture and even the hunting pictures on the walls exactly as she'd found them when she'd arrived. It was the most comfortable room she'd occupied since leaving Foxcomb Hall, her family's estate, four years ago, but far more formal and elaborate than her bedroom at Ruth's had been. Richard had encouraged her to redecorate it. Perhaps it was finally time to learn to properly decorate a room. It was a skill she'd never mastered. Her mother had never been allowed to choose anything except the menus at Foxcomb Hall and even these had come under her father's irritating scrutiny. 'Tomorrow you and I can go shopping for some different fabric for the curtains.'

'That would be lovely, a nice shade of blue, perhaps.' Mrs Parker eyed the room as if she'd had plans for it for some time and could at last set them in motion. Mary didn't mind.

'But no chintz. I detest chintz.' Her father had made Foxcomb Hall awash in it.

'So do I.' Mrs Parker winked in solidarity, then looked about with a disapproving tut. 'Let me see where that maid has got to with the water. I like the girl, but she's gone too long without a proper lady to serve. It's made her forgetful.' Mrs Parker bustled out of the room in search of the errant pitcher and basin.

A proper lady.

Mary was surprised Mrs Parker had said so. She'd walked in on Mary crying over the last letter from Mary's sister, Jane, and Mary had told her everything, needing a friend and the comfort that Ruth had once provided. Not since those first few weeks with Ruth had Mary felt so lonely and far from the family she once thought had loved her. Mrs Parker had proven as sympathetic as Ruth and Richard, not judging or blaming her for having been young and in love and too naive to understanding the consequences of her decisions. It gave her some hope that others in America would be as forgiving, but after her parents' shameful behaviour, it was a thin hope.

No one here besides those two will ever know. Richard had assured her that there were too many people with questionable histories of their own that they'd conveniently left behind when they'd come to the States to chase their dreams of success and freedom to worry about hers. Mary hoped that was true.

Mary sat at the dressing table where her ribbons, sewing box, stationery and other personal effects had been arranged. These little things were the only effort she'd made to bring any of herself into the room. She moved aside a small book of poetry and studied the letter she'd written on the fine paper beneath it. It was to her mother and father to let them know where she was living, but, try as she might to finish it, seal it and send it, she couldn't. They'd stopped caring about where she was or what she was doing four years ago. The only one who cared was Jane. Her letters sat tied with a blue ribbon in the top drawer, her longing to see her sister again and share everything that had happened since they'd last been together dripping from each finely formed word. These letters were the only thing Mary ever received from her family, from the only family member who had cared enough to defy their father to correspond with Mary.

Mary took the thickest letter from Jane out of the drawer and opened it to read again about Jane's wedding at St George's London last year. Her sister described the cream satin of her dress, the fine lace of her train, the music, guests and every detail of the dishes served at the wedding breakfast. It was everything that would have been Mary's if she hadn't been so weak and stupid, if she'd followed her head instead of her heart. It was a mistake she would never make again.

The jingle of equipage and the snort of horses on the kerb outside drew Mary to the window. She pushed aside the curtain to see the black-lacquered top of Mr Fairclough's carriage glistening with the carriage lamps affixed to the sides. The front door opened, spilling light into the street as Mr Fairclough crossed the pavement with sure, firm steps that made the edges of his cape flutter. His head was bent down, tilting his top hat at an angle of contemplation made obvious when he stopped outside the carriage door to raise a hand in goodbye to Richard. It was the same motion Mary had made when bidding the servants at Ruth's cottage goodbye after Mary had overseen the packing up, selling and dispersing of Ruth's things according to her will. The rest had been sent on to Richard to be absorbed into the various rooms of his house. Every once in a while Mary noticed them, pausing to think that they shouldn't be here, she shouldn't be here but in the London Jane described.

Fool. You were such a fool. She crumpled the letter and let a tear of anger and self-pity slip down her cheek before she roughly wiped it away. It all could have been different if she'd chosen better, but she hadn't and it'd cost her everything: her family, her heart, her future, her life and all the things about it that she'd loved.

Mary watched Mr Fairclough climb into the carriage. She could see nothing of him through the dark window at the back, but if even one of his thoughts turned to her and what Richard had suggested she hoped it was favourable. The driver snapped the reins and the clop of the horse's hooves echoed off the cobbles as the vehicle carried him away. She'd listened to Mr Fairclough tonight speaking in her native accent about ideas and prospects, the future and plans for himself and the business, and she'd been impressed. She wanted to be like him, to come from nothing and make something of herself. Marriage to a man of his standing and potential could help her achieve that goal. If she put as much effort into herself and this matter as he did his railroads, the future she'd once imagined for herself could be hers again. She would be a married woman, even if she knew very little about the man she was setting her sights on.

Not a difficult problem to rectify, she could hear Richard say, and it wasn't.

She hadn't been expected to marry for love when she'd come out in England. There was no reason to allow love to be the guiding force in a match here either. After all, her parents had supposedly loved her, but they hadn't hesitated to cast her out of their lives. Preston had sworn to love her, but he'd abandoned her the moment he'd had the chance. Only Ruth had loved her and death had stolen her away, leaving Mary to grieve as deeply as she had in that dirty inn on the lonely road to Gretna Green. Mary refused to allow love to guide her or to shatter her or her world again. Her last attempt at marriage had been the wild imaginings of a lovesick girl struck dumb by infatuation. Her next marriage would be one of sense and rational thought, of a partnership with a man she respected who could make her a true lady once again.

Chapter Two

December 1842

'Here you are.' Silas dusted and dried the ink of his signature and handed it across the desk to Mr Hachman, his man of affairs. Outside his office door, and down the stairs, the whir of machines in the Baltimore Southern machine shop made a steady hum, broken now and again by the metal clink of hammers pounding steel into the parts and pieces needed to build and maintain a railroad. This machine shop was the first of what Silas hoped would be many to come. Soon they and numerous station houses would dot the landscapes of Baltimore and cities across the States, helping ferry people and the mass of goods entering Baltimore's ports up and down the coast.

'Congratulations, Mr Fairclough, on your first delivery of steel railway tracks from your, I mean the Baltimore Southern's, new foundry.' Mr Hachman collected the signed papers and slid them into his leather portfolio. 'The regular deliveries will keep the men employed here and on the tracks busy for ages.'

'Good, for there are a great many men in need of jobs.' The country hadn't entirely recovered after the panic of 1837 and with cotton prices still low, there were many men in need of work. Silas and his railroad would give it to them. He touched the signet ring on his left little finger. His father had once accused Silas of not possessing a charitable enough spirit, of being greedy and grasping, but he wasn't; he simply pursued charity in a different manner than his father. After all, there was nothing wrong with helping one's self while helping others. It didn't all have to be privation. 'We'll dominate the American market and never have our progress hampered by the Atlantic Ocean or foreign politics again.'

'It is a grand day, Mr Fairclough, and a grand future for you and Mr Jackson.'

'All we need now is the new English engine to haul more goods and people over our freshly laid tracks.'

We also need Richard to remain well enough to see everything come to fruition.

Silas flicked a speck off the green-velvet blotter. The rattle in Richard's lungs had grown worse with the cold weather. The ever-increasing progress of his disease was too much like the month the typhoid had crept through his family's London neighbourhood while everyone waited to see if they or someone they loved developed the fever. The question for the Faircloughs had been answered when Silas's father had fallen ill. The determination, energy and spirit that had carried his father through a hundred difficulties with the Foundation hadn't been enough to fight off the disease and he'd passed, leaving so much for Silas to carry, just as Richard would. Silas swivelled his chair around to peer out the large window behind him at the packed dirt of the Baltimore Southern rail yard. The landscape was made starker by the grey clouds hanging low in the sky and the bare trees dotting the edge of the property. He was prepared to take over the management of the railway, but he didn't want it in this manner just as he hadn't wanted his father to die. He wouldn't disappoint Richard in the end the way he'd disappointed his father.

'Mr Fairclough, there's another matter of some concern that I must discuss with you,' Mr Hachman said, halting Silas's melancholy turn. 'Our English solicitor called on your mother and was informed that the Fairclough Foundation has not received their usual monthly drafts for the last six months.'

'How is that possible?' Silas swivelled around to face his manager. 'I personally sign those bank drafts and include a letter with them every month.'

'I don't know. This was all the solicitor sent concerning the matter.' Mr Hachman removed a paper from his portfolio and handed it to Silas.

Silas read the man's brief account of his conversation with Silas's mother in October. He jumped to his feet, flinging the letter down on his desk. 'This is two months old.'

'It was sent by packet ship which was delayed in Liverpool while they waited for the hold to be filled.'

'Given what we pay him to represent our interests in England, he should've had the wherewithal to send this by Cunard steamer.'

'I've sent word that all future correspondence regarding any Baltimore Southern or Fairclough family business is to be sent the fastest way possible.'

'But what about this?' His stomach knotted at the prospect of his family going without or enduring financial straits due to this unexplained delay. If he hadn't been so preoccupied with the foundry, he might have kept a better eye on the regular payments instead of leaving it to others. He could have stopped this problem before it had even become one.

'I've received no follow-up correspondence since this letter. Our solicitor, having heard nothing from us, may have assumed the issue was resolved or is still waiting for additional instructions.'

'I wonder why one of my sisters didn't write to tell me there was a problem.' They'd never been shy about describing the most trivial details of their lives and delighting over any description of his, cheering him on from afar. He had no idea what his mother thought of his life in America. The few letters she'd sent to him over the years had been terse in regards to whatever business had forced her to break her missive silence. He couldn't blame her for not putting pen to paper more often. He hadn't given her a great deal of reason to write to him when he'd left England.

'I can't say, sir, but if you have any other channels through which to investigate the matter, I suggest you employ them.'

'I'll send a letter to Lady Alexandra, my father's cousin. She's on good terms with my mother. If they're in trouble she'll know about it. Arrange for a bank draft to include with the letter. I want it sent by steamer immediately.'

'Yes, Mr Fairclough.' The man clapped closed his leather folder, collected his things and left.

Silas laid a piece of paper on the blotter and, in very concise terms so as not to create a panic where there might not be one, but also to stress the urgency of the situation, wrote to Lady Alexandra. Silas prayed his mother would turn to Lady Alexandra for help if things were truly dire, but he knew the strength of the Fairclough pride. His father used to say that Silas possessed an overabundance of it, just like the Earl, his grandfather.

It can't be that bad. If it were, Lady Alexandra would have written to me about it at once.

The fact that he had not received a concerned letter from her or either of his sisters gave him some hope. Perhaps there was already a letter on the way stating that all was well and the bank drafts had been received and cashed.

It'd been a long time since he'd communicated with Lady Alexandra and as he dusted the letter and prepared it for the inclusion of the draft, he thought of the Christmases that he and his family had spent at the grand dame's manor house. His sisters might not have cared to spend time at Lady Alexandra's estate, but Silas had been mesmerised by her lavish life, stately house, manners, servants and the bit of port she used to slip him after dinner. Time with her had been his first taste of true prosperity and he'd appreciated it, especially the Christmas after his father had passed.

When was the last time I was home for Christmas?

He couldn't remember. It was long before Liverpool. During the last few years, the railroad's affairs had made it impossible for him to travel. He summoned his clerk and gave him the letter for Mr Hachman. The attorney was one of the best man of affairs Silas had ever worked with and he reminded Silas of Septimus Clarke, the Fairclough Foundation's general manager who'd helped see it through the difficult years following Silas's father's death. He was the same man who'd convinced his mother to find a place for Silas in Liverpool with Jasper King, placing Silas on the path that had led him to Richard and finally to success.

Silas wondered if his mother cursed her decision to let him go to Liverpool all those years ago, especially since Septimus had retired. Millie had written to Silas about Jerome Edwards, the new manager who'd been engaged to take Septimus's place. She'd spoken highly of him, but Silas regretted not having been there to help interview him and other prospective candidates, to at last put his business skills to use for his family and show his mother that his natural gifts had real value. Instead, he'd trusted from afar that his mother and sisters had made the right decision, just as he'd trusted that the monthly payments had reach them. They hadn't.

The door to Silas's office opened and Richard strode in with confident steps but there was no mistaking now the looseness in his suit or the hollowness in his cheeks. Silas touched the signet ring with his thumb, his heart dropping even while he smiled. 'Richard, what brings you here?'

'I want to see the plans for the new English locomotive you've been telling me about.'

'It's magnificent.' Silas laid out a number of drawings of the English-built locomotive that had been sent to him during his correspondence with Mr Williams, the engine's designer. They were drawn in a fine hand with strong lines and a view from every angle. 'It uses half the amount of coal as our current model and is stronger and faster. With this engine we can reduce travel times and haul twice the freight. Between this and the new track, we'll surpass our competition.'

'I have no doubt it will be as successful as our foundry.' He clapped Silas on the back, the heavy fall of his hand much lighter than before. 'Let's go for a walk and you can show me the new steam works.'

They left the relative quiet of the office for the clatter and banging of the machine shop. Silas and Richard called out and replied to greetings from the workers whose faces were blackened by sweat and grease. Silas and Richard's dark suits were a stark contrast to the men's stained shirts and sturdy trousers. Outside, the musty scent of coal from the large deposits elsewhere on the grounds carried on the light breeze. It mingled with the dampness from the nearby Patapsco River that flowed out into the Atlantic, its waters crowded with ships hauling goods and rough materials in and out of Baltimore harbour.

They walked across the rail yard to a tall new building of glass and iron being constructed near the tracks. Men moved about the metal structure, heaving the large panes of glass into place. 'I doubled the size of the steam works to accommodate the increased width of the English engine and added more glass for better light for the workers. It's a bit of a gamble, but it'll be worth it when the first steam engine rolls out of here and we're turning a profit instead of sinking money into it.'

'I'm glad to see our plans progressing, although the credit for this one is entirely due to you.' Richard waved his walking stick at the organised chaos around them, then fixed on Silas. 'With so much settled, have you given the matter of matrimony any further consideration?'

'I have not.' This last week was the most time Silas had spent in Baltimore since September. He'd travelled between Baltimore and Pennsylvania to oversee the acquisition of the foundry and the conversion of the steel works into producing rails. On the rare occasion when he had been in town, meetings with businessmen and investors had left him little time to enjoy the quiet of his home much less Richard's, or the pleasantries of courting Lady Mary.

'I still say it's a strong proposal. You won't have to waste time courting flibbertigibbets and she won't have to parade herself in front of society bachelors who'll size up what I intend to settled on her and see if it's enough to make them overlook everything else.'

'What everything else?'

'I'll leave that to the lady to tell you. I'm not

her father, simply someone who's concerned about her future and happiness, and yours. I want you both to have a true partner, not someone who'll only see the advantage in the other and then turn cold once that advantage is no longer a benefit.'

'I thought this entire idea was to my and Lady Mary's advantage.' Silas laughed as they strolled towards the dock where the ship unloaded the coal, the scent of it and the grease mingling with the faint mist of steam from the nearby engines.

'It is and I'm convinced the two of you are companionable. Speak to her tonight at Mrs Penniman's Christmastime Ball. Try to see in her what I see and what she can offer you. If you can't, then I won't hold it against you if you decline.'

And he wouldn't. Silas was sure of it. Richard might propose an idea, but in the end the final decision always remained with Silas. It was time to evaluate this investment and make a decision and settle the matter one way or another.

Chapter Three

Mary sat across from Richard in the carriage, her yellow-silk ball gown pressed in by Mrs Parker who sat beside her. They waited in the long queue of vehicles inching towards the Pennimans' front door. Christmas was still three weeks away but the Pennimans' Christmastime Ball marked the start of the festive season in Baltimore and the round of parties before everyone secluded themselves with their families to celebrate the season. The Pennimans' Mount Vernon Square house was built in the classical style with wide columns flanking a massive wooden front door. It stood with a number of equally impressive homes surrounding the wide, tree-filled square at the centre of which stood a tall Doric column topped with a statue of President George Washington.

'You spoke to Mr Fairclough again about your idea, didn't you?' Mary asked Richard, struggling to sit still on the squabs as the carriage moved forward, then stopped. Foundry business had kept Mr Fairclough away from Baltimore for so long that Mary was afraid he'd forgotten about her. While he'd been gone, she'd purchased a new ball gown and two day dresses to make herself more appealing. She's been afraid to order more items, wanting to maintain some dignity should Mr Fairclough laugh off the idea of marrying her. Even if Mr Fairclough entertained the prospect, she didn't relish the ball being the first chance to broach the matter with him. There were too many things that could go wrong and ruin this venture before it even began. Mary had been thrilled when the invitation had arrived. She wasn't so thrilled now. It'd been years since she'd last attended a ball and she'd been a very different woman then, inexperienced and immature. She was none of those things tonight.

'I spoke with him.' Richard clasped the leather strap as the carriage shifted forward again.

'Was he amenable to the idea?' The promise of a sizeable inheritance should help him overlook her past mistakes, but she wanted to be loved for who she was, not how many dollars were in her bank account.

Love. Mary silently huffed, rapping her closed fan against her gloved palm. There was a notion she'd better dismiss. She'd placed her trust in love once before and it'd ruined her. She wouldn't make that mistake twice. If Richard believed Mr Fairclough was a good match for her, then that was enough reason for her to encourage the gentleman.

'He hasn't rejected it.'

'That's hardly comforting.'

'When it comes to Silas Fairclough, the lack of an outright rejection is good. He takes time to consider things. I've done my best to demonstrate the advantage of a union with you. It's up to you to close the deal.'

Mary resisted the urge to sigh. She'd been reduced to nothing more than a foundry to be negotiated and invested in. Well, it was better than being damaged goods that couldn't even be given away four years ago. She smoothed her gloved hands over her dress, wondering if she should have allowed the modiste to cut the bodice of the gown a touch lower. Mary had learned a long time ago what really caught a man's attention—there was no point in not advertising its availability to Mr Fairclough along with the potential for her more monetary assets. He might be thoughtful when it came to making decisions, but he was a still a man and, thankfully, a very nice-looking one with an admirable physique. She might not be pursuing him out of affection, but even she wasn't about to chase after any man, no matter how old or pudgy he was, simply because he might make her a wife. She wasn't so desperate yet.

'Don't worry, I'm sure you'll succeed. You have Silas's tenaciousness and good sense and he has your forgiving and kind-hearted nature, and both of you possess an eagerness for life that I admire. The two of you will get on well.'

'I hope so.' The future she wished to claim seemed to depend on it. Although she wasn't so certain she was as forgiving as Richard believed. The grudges she held against those still living across the ocean made the Rock of Gibraltar seem like a pebble in comparison. She took a deep breath and reached up to caress the watch, but it wasn't attached to her dress. She'd left it at home, but she pictured Ruth and the many hours she'd spent coaching Mary in patience and forgiveness, encouraging her to see past people's shortcomings. Mary had done her best to learn those lessons, but not even Ruth's influence had been enough to soften Mary's heart against her family. Mary adjusted the skirt of her dress, putting the old grievances aside. This ball was about claiming a different destiny than the one the people in England had chosen for her, not being bogged down by the past.

The carriage finally rolled up to the front walk and a footman opened the door. He offered Mary one gloved hand to help her down and she took it, Mr Fairclough momentarily forgotten in her eagerness to rush up the steps and into the light, music, voices and energy spilling from the house. There had been little life in the country with Ruth and a sedate and quiet one with Richard in Baltimore, but the self-imposed semi-seclusion which she'd endured for the past four years ended tonight. She would make her presence in Baltimore known in a way that even sitting at the head of Richard's table hadn't done. There would be no going back to anonymity after the ball and it terrified her as much as it thrilled her.

Richard escorted her inside and Mrs Parker following behind as expected of a respectable chaperon. In England, a lady's maid would never accompany her lady to a ball, but things in America were different and Mary was glad. She needed the comfort of friends around her tonight. Mary and Richard stepped into a rectangular hall with a black and white marble floor, white walls and more of the tall columns that had dominated the front of the house. They waded through the crush of people, Richard exchanging greetings with fellow businessmen while Mary smiled pleasantly at them. It wasn't long before they were in the receiving line and in front of the hosts.

'Lady Mary, it's a pleasure to have you here,' Mr Penniman greeted from where he stood beside his plump wife. 'May I introduce Mrs Penniman?'

Mary curtsied to their hostess, noting the fine flowers embroidered on the mauve silk of the other woman's ball gown and the massive diamonds encircling her wrists and throat. Mary's mother had once looked this radiant in her silks and family jewels and Mary had admired and coveted them the way she did Mrs Penniman's. If all went well tonight, she might enjoy such elegance again. It made her heart flutter as she rose, smiling respectfully at the matron who offered a beaming a smile in return.

'Lady Mary, you honour us with your presence. I never thought to have the daughter of an earl in my humble home.'

Mary's stomach tightened at the mention of her lineage and she braced herself, sure someone would step up to call her a fraud, but no one did, leaving it to her to make an impression on the hostess. 'Your home is as fine, if not finer, than most in Grosvenor Square and I'm delighted to be included in tonight's festivities.'

'Thank you so much, Lady Mary.'

Mary could see the matron sought as much approval as Mary did when it came to her efforts to entertain. She wondered from what humble roots Mrs Penniman had risen. She would have to ask Mrs Parker later.

The required pleasantries complete, Richard escorted Mary away from their hosts. They strolled through the high-ceilinged main hall with its white plaster and marble curving staircase leading up to the higher floors, past the ancient Roman sculptures and towards the large ballroom at the back of the house. It was slow going as they stopped every few feet for another meeting or introduction. Mary did her best to give her full attention to each new person, all the while aware of everyone around them. She was, without being too obvious, searching for Mr Fairclough.

When they finally extricated themselves from Mr and Mrs Baxter, who proved as eager as Mrs Penniman to meet Mary, Richard escorted her to the ballroom. The sight of it took her breath away. It was as impressive as any in England with a soaring-glass and wrought-iron ceiling. Tall columns interspersed with numerous windows dominated three of the four walls, allowing the city lights from outside to twinkle like the candles did in the chandeliers and sconces. On a raised dais at one end, the musicians played for the dancers who whirled and turned in their wide-skirted dresses and dark suits. It was everything she'd dearly loved once and that had comprised so much of her life, and everything she thought she would never delight in again. She longed to rush into the crowd, find a partner and enjoy the dances that had marked her Season in London before her life had collapsed but she remained beside Richard. She didn't want to crave it too much and have it all pulled away from her.

Without thinking, she glanced around, still searching for Mr Fairclough, eager to see him. A very small part of her, the one that had been tricked by Preston, stirred before she stamped it out. The idea that she was chasing after a man again frightened her, but this wasn't intended to be that sort of arrangement and she must be sensible and level headed in this matter. This was about a respectable marriage and a better future, not some clandestine tryst.

'I'll leave you two ladies here.' Richard, removed her hand from his arm. 'I'm off to the game room with the gentlemen.'

'So soon?' She hadn't imagined facing the ballroom without the surety of Richard's reputation to help bolster hers or to navigate the Mr Fairclough matter alone.

'I trust you'll be fine with Mrs Parker.'

'Don't worry, Mr Jackson, I'll watch out

for her as if she were my own daughter,' Mrs Parker assured him.

'I don't doubt you will. Ladies.' With a bow, he made for the smoky gambling room where the married gentlemen and confirmed bachelors would hole up for the evening, leaving the single men of marriageable age to the debutantes and their mothers.

Those debutantes and mothers watched Mary who pretended not to notice their curious scrutiny as she waded into the crowd. She and Mrs Parker stood on the edge of the dance floor as the dancers twirled by during the rousing reel. The young women's cheeks were flush with the thrill of the dance or the attention of the gentleman holding their hands. They were innocent in their white dresses of cascading ruffles accented with pink ribbons and bows and everything expected of well-bred young ladies, everything Mary no longer was. The men dancing with them gazed down at their simpering partners with an adoration verging on worship, as if they weren't worthy to hold the gloved hands of these fair maidens.

'I don't know how I'll compete with them for Mr Fairclough's attentions,' Mary said to

Mrs Parker. The dancing women were only a few years younger than her, but they didn't know disappointment, betrayal, shame and guilt as intimately as she did, and if they or their mothers knew the truth about Mary they'd promenade right out of the room to get away from her.

'Chin up, Lady Mary. You're a woman of experience, that's more than most of them can say, although I could point out the ones who could say it but I won't, at least not yet. You need to meet them first.' She winked and Mary stifled a laugh.

'Are you suggesting that they aren't as innocent as they look?'

'Most people aren't, that's a good rule for anyone to remember, especially you who has suffered enough for her mistakes and doesn't deserve any more.' Mrs Parker slipped her hand in Mary's and gave it a comforting squeeze.

'Thank you, Mrs Parker, that means a great deal to me.'

'Smile, Lady Mary, and look merry, you have a man to catch.' Mrs Parker levelled her hand towards the opposite side of the dance floor. There, Mr Fairclough stood with a young woman on either side of him. They peered up at him with eyes so round it was a wonder he didn't fall into them. He smiled in delight at their adoration, making Mary want to gag. She'd seen that expression on a hundred young ladies' faces during her Season, their hopeful mothers standing behind them wondering if they'd found a real catch. It was all an act she knew well. They wanted Mr Fairclough for nothing more than his money. They had no real interest in him, although Mary wasn't certain her reasons for pursuing him were any more noble than theirs.

'What do you think of Richard's proposal of me and Mr Fairclough?' Mary's judgement had failed her once before. It was time to rely on other people's more clearheaded opinions.

'I've known him since he arrived in Baltimore and I haven't a bad thing to say about him. My brother is the foreman at his machine shop and all the workers there speak highly of him, too. He's good to his employees, paying poor Mr Stone who was sick and has three children at home who would have starved if his pay had been withheld. Unlike some of these hard-hearted businessmen in here who care only for profits, Mr Fairclough takes care of his workers. I think Mr Jackson is right, the two of you will suit, but not if you lose him to one of those gadflies flitting about him.' Mrs Parker set her plump shoulders, hidden beneath the lines of her dark blue dress devoid of all ruffles and frills, and faced Mary. 'Come. It's time to shoo them away.'

'Yes, it is.' Bolstered by Mrs Parker's support, Mary took hold of the sides of her skirt and accompanied her companion around the edge of the ballroom towards Mr Fairclough.

The music ended and couples entered and left the dance floor. The change in partners made Mary walk faster, afraid Mr Fairclough would escort one of those fawning women out for the next dance and give the little vixen a chance to snare him. Mary wasn't about to lose out on becoming a wife just because, like the horses to Gretna Green, she hadn't been quick enough. If she and Preston had arrived at the anvil a day or even a few hours sooner, it would have all been done, and then everything that had happened afterwards wouldn't have mattered. She wouldn't have been cast aside because she would have been wed.

'Mr Fairclough, you promised me the next dance,' Mary announced, stepping between him and one young woman and catching Mrs Parker's congratulatory smile from where she stood just behind him. The women flanking him all but sneered at Mary. It wasn't their reaction she cared about, but Mr Fairclough's. He could easily laugh at her the way Preston had while she'd lain in the inn's old bed, still in pain, asking if they'd continue on to Gretna Green when she felt better. Then he'd walked out the door, leaving her to the hard innkeeper's wife who'd demanded payment from her father for the stained sheets and what little care she'd offered Mary. When her father had returned from paying the greedy woman, things had become far worse than she could have imagined when the bleeding had first started in the carriage or when Preston's back had faded down the inn's dark hall.

The memory of it nearly made Mary mumble her apologies and flee into the crowd, but she stood her ground. She wasn't about to run, not with the mothers whispering about

Mary's forwardness. They must wonder who this young woman was who wasn't a debutante judging by her dress and wasn't married either given her bare ring finger. She shouldn't have asked him to dance—it wasn't done—but she'd made her statement and there was no backing down from it.

Mary's stiff stance softened when Mr Fairclough's surprise changed into delight. 'You're right, Lady Mary, I'd forgotten. Can you forgive me?'

The Lady before her name silenced the mothers and their daughters who gazed on Mary with more respect than they'd shown when she'd first trounced between them and the object of their hunt. If only her title had guaranteed her this much respect back home.

'How could I hold such a small oversight against you?' she answered with a graciousness to impress even herself.

'If you ladies will excuse me?' He offered Mary his arm and she took it, allowing him to escort her to the dance floor.

'That was quite a bold invitation to dance,' Mr Fairclough complimented as he laid one hand on her waist and faced her for the Viennese Waltz. Mary would have preferred a gallop or a vigorous polka to these slow steps, but she hadn't exactly given either of them a choice. She'd simply demanded a partner. She was getting what she'd asked for.

'I've learned the hard way that tarrying can lose one many opportunities.'

'So have I. One does not form companies and forge ahead with a railroad by being shy.'

'Nor does a woman secure a dance by standing near a wall.'

'Something tells me you aren't in the habit of standing by walls, Lady Mary.'

'I've held up my fair share of them.' Too many in the last four years, not that she and Ruth had ever attended anything like a dance, but if they had, Mary would have done all she could to fade into the decorations. Standing out in London had landed her in the worst trouble of her life. Even now apprehension made her steps a little heavier. She'd been this forward with Preston, triumphant at having snatched him away from the other ladies, but that achievement had been no victory in the end. She wondered if she'd failed to really learn from her mistakes, but Mr Fairclough was nothing like Preston. This man had built himself up through hard work instead of resting on the family laurels. 'But not any more.'

'Good.'

Silas turned them in time to the swaying melody of the music. The slow movement allowed him to admire the woman in his arms and the stunning change that had come over her since the last time he'd seen her. She wasn't dressed in the white and cream satins of the other ladies her age, but she wasn't swathed in plain grey or black either. She wore a yellow silk gown overlaid with a netting of fine red roses. The waist of the dress was cut in tight to her natural form, the bodice sloping down to reveal the barest hint of the tops of her breasts. Her slender arms, curved to match the angle of his and the dance, were covered in long, white gloves that complemented the dress, all of it whispering of mature elegance, taste and wealth. She was without jewellery, but her hair was pulled off her face and neck and arranged in small ringlets that shivered with each dance step. 'Even if you wished to fade into the drapery, you're too much of an interest to everyone to allow them to forget you or your daring dance invitation.'

An enticing pink spread across Lady Mary's cheeks, bringing a glow to her smooth skin that heightened the one created by the warmth of the ballroom. 'I'm sorry for my unconventional request. It wasn't my intention to make a spectacle of either of us.'

'Make a spectacle of us. It's to your advantage and mine.' The other women had simpered and whined at his sides. She'd stood in front of him and made her intentions clear. It was an admirable trait that could serve the wife of a businessman well. There would be no guessing what she wanted or needed. Her flaunting of convention was also intriguing. A man who wanted to succeed had to think differently when everyone else was doing the same thing. It was clear she was aware that doing something different could get results. After all, it was she dancing with him instead of either of those two women who'd been hanging on his every boring word. However, one dance wasn't enough to make him drop on his knee and propose. What Richard was suggesting could influence the rest of his life and he would take as much time as necessary to decide as he did with any other venture, unless she proposed first. It wouldn't surprise him if she did.

'You want to be spoken about?' she asked.

'Better spoken about than ignored.'

'I've never found either choice to be particularly endearing.' She slid a hard glance at the young ladies who'd been angling for his attention where they stood whispering together while they watched Silas and Mary dance.

'I suppose that depends on one's station in society. You're new so people are curious about you. It'll make you a much sought-after guest and lend you an aura of mystery that people will scramble to delve.'

'Or they'll create stories to fill in the gaps.'

'Not if you give them stories to take home first.'

'I'm sure the gentlemen at the dinner took home enough of an impression of me for their wives.'

'Men are useless there.'

'You're right. My brother, Peter, could never be counted on for news of a new neighbour.' Her smile faded to the same sorrowful look that sometimes came over her when he saw her at Richard's. 'Of course he was vocal enough when it was of no benefit to me.'

He didn't ask what it was her brother had said. He'd heard about enough disappointed fathers and brothers from the women at the Foundation to guess. He wondered if his mother spoke of him in the same disillusioned terms. He'd sneaked away from England without telling her, eager to follow his dreams while disappointing hers. Silas straightened. He had as much right to lead the life he wanted as his mother and father had and his parents should have understood this. His father hadn't thought twice about turning his back on his own father and the naval career he'd laid out for him to establish the Foundation. However, when it had come to his own son trying to strike out on his own, he'd been nothing but critical and his mother had carried on in the same vein after his passing. 'But he isn't here and we are and we must make the best of this magnificent evening.'

'I already am. It's been ages since I've danced and with the most charming and clever man in the room.' She tilted her head and offered a smile that could charm the shoes off a horse, the same one that had helped convince the rich men around Richard's table to break convention and drink and discuss business in a lady's presence.

'But tonight you must truly shine.'

'Must I?'

'Don't tell me a woman who marched up to a man and demanded a dance doesn't want to stand out?'

'I see I can't lie to you.'

'There's no reason to.'

'I don't suppose there is.'

'Good, then let's plan our strategy because the dance will soon be over and I don't want the flock of women who were with me before learning anything from you about being assertive.' He glanced at the young women he'd abandoned to dance with Lady Mary. They watched him with anticipation, almost counting out the number of stanzas left until they could have another crack at him.

'We can't have that, now can we?' Lady Mary stepped closer to him as if staking her claim. Her confidence in getting what she wanted was intriguing as was her new look this evening for there was no mistaking it was for him. Whatever Richard had proposed to her, she'd taken to the idea with a fervour. It boded well for a woman who might have to join Silas in the promotion of a number of ideas that many, including the fine owner of this house, would call insane. Some of those ideas might fail and he would have to move on to others. He guessed by her decision to come to America that Lady Mary was capable of moving on from failure instead of allowing it to destroy her. 'What shall we do first?'

'Introductions, lots of them and to the right ladies, those are key to successfully launching you.' It was something Richard would have seen to in the first weeks of her arrival, but as he'd confided to Silas, it was the lady's objections that had stopped him. Silas was glad to see that she'd changed her mind.

'Whatever magic you intend to work, I ask you do so without mentioning my family connections.'

'A difficult promise to make given your title.'

'Then mention it as infrequently as you can. I'll stand on my own merits or none at all.'

'You've set quite a challenge for me.'

'You can live up to it.'

'I'll surpass it.'

'Like breeching etiquette to steal a man for a dance?'

'No, like this.' He swung her off the dance floor and they stopped before Mrs Wilson, another grand dame of Baltimore society whose husband had been at the dinner.

'Mrs Wilson, have you had the pleasure of meeting Lady Mary?' The ladies exchanged greetings before Silas continued. 'She is one of the most renowned whist players in England.'

Mary threw Silas a questioning look he ignored. He had no idea if she played cards, but this was her entrée into a party. It was up to her to take it and she did. 'Yes, I'm an excellent player.'

'Then you must come to my card party Thursday night.' Mrs Wilson trilled her fingers together in delight. 'We could do with a little cage rattling of my regular attendees, but I must warn you that we play for higher stakes than most ladies are accustomed to.'

'Good, it makes the game so much more interesting.'

'Then I'll send the invitation tomorrow.'

Before Mrs Wilson could say anything more, Silas politely guided Lady Mary away, in search of their next conquest.

'I'll have to practise card games with Mrs Parker before Thursday.'

'Don't practise too much. You'll endear yourself to Mrs Wilson more if you lose to her. For a wealthy woman she's quite the penny-pincher.'

'I can feel my pin-money purse growing lighter as we speak.'

The rest of the ball passed in much the same way, with Silas leading Mary from one matron or businessman to another and making the introductions. Some introductions were sedate while others were as outlandish as her ability to play whist. She never objected to any of his more creative introductions, but went along with them, not chiding him afterwards, even when he'd boasted of her having a very distant family connection to Queen Victoria. She craved position as much as he and, like him, she'd welcomed each opportunity he offered to increase hers, meeting every expectation he'd set and amazing him as no other woman had before.

* * *

'For someone who didn't like gaining attention you picked up on the game very quickly,' Silas complimented as he escorted Lady Mary through the main hall towards the front door, the large clock at the base of the stairs ringing twice to mark the late hour.

'I'm a fast learner.'

'With a very full social calendar.' So much so that he wondered if she would have time to see him again. The musicians were playing the last song and most of the guests were making their way to their carriages and some much-needed rest after what was for Silas the first ball he'd enjoyed in ages.

'Did you have a good time, Lady Mary?' Richard asked when they reached the front hall, Mrs Parker beside them. The matron had proved herself a reliable, respectable and discreet shadow throughout the evening.

'I had a marvellous time.' Mary's excitement was the greatest compliment she could have paid to Silas.

A footman stepped forward with her cloak and Silas took if from the man and held it up for her to slip into. She turned, eyeing him over her shoulder, the scintillating look of experience and mischief making Silas's hand tighten on the velvet. She'd enjoyed tonight as much as he and regretted parting, too. He set the cloak on her shoulders, resisting the urge to caress the bare skin on the back of her neck with his fingertips, to see her full lips part in surprise at the gesture. He'd proven himself a trustworthy partner tonight. He didn't wish to scare her off by acting like a cad.

She faced him as she tied the laces of the cloak, the black velvet heightening the flush of her cheeks and the sparkle illuminating her eyes. Silas had never noticed how brown they were until this moment. He couldn't help but think that with a rich bronze-coloured silk cloak trimmed in white fur she would shine brighter than all the debutantes in their white lace and pink ribbons. She was young and pretty, and although he'd never allowed either of those traits to trick him into a decision before, it was a tempting combination tonight. The businessman in him saw the advantage of the union, while the man in him wanted to taste a little more than her investment potential.

Silas offered her his arm and they walked

together behind Mrs Parker and Richard to the carriage. Their breath mingled in small clouds over their heads before disappearing into the dark night. They didn't speak about the evening, but enjoyed the comfortable quiet of each other's presence until they reached the carriage. They waited together while Richard and Mrs Parker settled inside, the prospect of bidding her goodnight bothering Silas more than his not having visited the game room to woo investors. When it was at last her turn, Silas handed her in, savouring the weight of her small hand in his and the pressure of it against his palm. Reluctantly, he released her and closed the carriage door, but before he could step back and let it drive away she lowered the window. 'Thank you for a very interesting evening. I look forward to seeing you tomorrow.'

'Am I seeing you tomorrow?'

'Most definitely.' She slid him a sly smile that made his fingers itch to trace her full lips, her confidence as enticing as her dictate. 'At three, we're having tea together.'

'It's been a long time since I've had a proper English tea.'

'Until tomorrow, then.' With a suggestive nod, she sat back from the window, the faint outline of her in the carriage lantern barely visible as the driver urged the horse into a walk and the carriage rolled away.

With Mary gone, the winter chill settled over him, one her presence beside him this evening had kept at bay. If he went through with this, he would be taking on the responsibilities of a wife and family. He wasn't adverse to the task for there were hundreds of workers already dependent on him and the Baltimore Southern for their livelihoods. He would never knowingly betray their trust or fail to take care of them, yet he'd failed his family once before. With the bank notes not reaching home he was failing them again. The possibility that Lady Mary might come to rely on him for something he wasn't capable of giving or ask him to be someone he wasn't the way his parents had done cemented his feet to the cold pavement. It wasn't until another carriage pulled up to the kerb and a young couple came forward to climb into it that Silas began the slow walk back inside the Pennimans' house.

There was no need to worry. During their

time together tonight Lady Mary had made it clear that she understood the kind of man he was and his ambitions and desires. She would not look down on his pursuit of business and success the way his father had, but do all she could to help him in his efforts to achieve it.

Back inside the warmth of the Pennimans' house, Silas greeted a number of his investors with enthusiastic words and smiles, his success surrounding him like the chill of the night. These reminders of his success bolstered his faith in himself and he vowed that even though he'd failed as a son, he would not fail as a husband and some day a father.

Chapter Four

'How do you think he'll propose?' Mrs Parker asked Mary as they strolled through Richard's side garden. They were enjoying a rare fine day in the midst of cold ones as winter tightened its grip on Maryland. Despite being up late last night, Mary had barely slept, unable to think about anything but Mr Fairclough and their time together. It'd been a delightful evening and she'd been loath to part with him, her heart racing as she'd all but forced him to join her for tea today, but she hadn't been able to let him go without some expectation of seeing him again.

This is about securing your future and nothing else, she reminded herself for the hundredth time since she'd crawled into bed last night.

The excitement that ran like a current under all thoughts of him and their time together was nothing more than discovering that there was genuine affability between them and that on his arm she'd once again been a young girl full of hope and promise who believed in the future. It hurt to imagine losing the chance to experience it again because she'd failed to capture his attention, except she hadn't, she was sure of it. When he'd escorted her to the carriage, the look he'd given her and the way his hand had lingered in hers had struck her deep. She and Silas had been partners last night and he'd treated her with more respect than anyone else ever had. Not even Preston at his most charming moments had been so captivating, honest or genuine with her as Mr Fairclough, but she didn't wish to get her hopes up as she'd done before and have it all fall to pieces.

'He won't propose. It's too soon.' Mr Fairclough was a man of action but he wasn't about to act so quickly in something this important. Mary knew the folly and regret that came with rushing towards marriage, but she also knew the dangers of dallying. She was sure Mr Fairclough did, too, although which course of action he decided to take in this matter remained to be seen. Either way, Mary had dressed accordingly, donning one of her two new day gowns and some jewellery to make herself as appealing as possible. This tea was another chance to catch his eye, one she could not miss, especially given what she'd decided to tell him today. The truth could ruin everything, so better it do so now than after days or weeks of courting.

'Oh, he'll propose all right and he'll do it today,' Mrs Parker assured her, increasing Mary's anticipation even while the rational part of her warned her against getting her hopes up. 'I saw the two of you together last night and the way he looked at you. You've captured his interest and a man like him will snap you up.'

'You make me sound like the purchase of a new foundry for his railroad.'

'He'll approach it that way so don't expect roses and candies, but he'll turn you into a queen one way or another.'

'I'm hardly queen material, and once he finds out the truth, for I'll have to tell him, who knows how he'll react.' Despite the risk to this venture, she didn't want him to hear the story from someone else.

'Mr Fairclough won't judge you as harshly as you think. I don't know all of his past, but some of the things I've heard him say to Mr Jackson makes me think he's made enough mistakes of his own to not judge you for yours.'

She wanted to believe that, but she'd seen how cruel and callous men could be. Even her father and brother had turned their backs on her. Her brother had accused her of ruining his chance for a union with Lord Breckenridge's daughter. Mary thought the young woman should have sent her a thank-you note for saving her from a loveless future. Her brother had wanted Lord Breckenridge's daughter's money more than he'd wanted the woman, making his and their father's rage against Mary and her mistake even more severe. She was sure Mr Fairclough was interested in her for more than what she might one day inherit, but it didn't mean he wished to assume the taint of her past. She had to allow him to decide whether or not to continue to pursue her so he could never say she'd tried to pull the wool over his eyes or resent her for trapping him in a questionable union.

The voice of a driver calling to the carriage

horses to stop carried over the garden wall. A moment later Mr Fairclough's hearty greeting to Richard's butler followed. Mr Fairclough exchanged a few pleasant words with the man as he always did instead of ignoring him as if he was nothing more than a potted plant the way her father used to do with the Foxcomb servants.

Mary froze on the gravel path, wanting to rush into the house and up the front stairs to her room before Mr Fairclough could see her, but she didn't. She would face whatever was going to happen today and move forward with her life one way or another. 'It's time to find out exactly what kind of man Mr Fairclough is.'

Silas warmed his hands over the sitting-room fire. The room held a decidedly masculine air, with heavy wood trim and leather decor and more weapons than watercolours on the walls. It was a bachelor's idea of decoration if Silas had ever seen one. Silas had come straight here from the metal shop and listening to Mr Kent's ideas for a new kind of steel rail, one that would support the larger

English-designed engine once Silas acquired the patent and began manufacturing it. Except it wasn't building more powerful steam engines in America that had Silas standing on his toes. He'd been up a great many hours last night after the ball, thinking about Lady Mary. She had proven herself an intriguing investment and Silas refused to sit idle and wait once a decision was made. However, if there was one thing Silas knew about women after growing up with two sisters and his mother, they did not wish to be treated like commodities. It would be a delicate balancing act to present a reasonable argument for why they should form a partnership while appearing like a genuinely besotted suitor. He couldn't swoon too much because Lady Mary would instantly see through that ruse. It would tarnish whatever credibility he'd established at the ball and deny him a better taste of the vixen who'd pinned him with a look to heat his blood over her shoulder last night. That side of Lady Mary had intrigued him more than he cared to admit. He was intent on approaching this deal rationally, but the intensity of her reaction to him and what it meant if she accepted him stirred all the irrational parts of him. He wasn't sure how he would achieve this delicate balance between business and pleasure and there was no more time to think about it as Lady Mary and Mrs Parker entered the room.

'Good afternoon,' Lady Mary greeted with a politeness that failed to cover the spark of anticipation in her expression.

'How nice to see you, Mr Fairclough,' Mrs Parker offered in her perpetually cheery voice while she helped Lady Mary off with her coat.

'Good afternoon, ladies.' Silas bowed to the women, almost falling over at the sight of Lady Mary's gown. For a chilly day, she wore a daringly low-cut dress of champagne-coloured satin that was fitted to her waist and decorated with faint embroidery in a darker thread around the wide neck that revealed the tops of her full breasts. Those particular assets were made more noticeable by the small watch on a gold chain hung beneath the curve of the right one. There was no missing that she'd chosen that dress to tempt him. It was working. Silas straightened, adjusting his cravat as he did.

Rational. You must remain somewhat rational.

'How is the new foundry doing?' Mrs

Parker asked, as welcoming and informal with him as she'd always been whenever he visited Richard's. Long before she'd become Lady Mary's lady's maid, she'd been the house-keeper here. During Silas's early days in Baltimore, she'd been a motherly figure to him at a time when he'd been very much without family.

'Producing steel rails exactly as expected.'

'Congratulations to you, Mr Fairclough.' Mrs Parker nudged her young charge with her elbow. 'There's nothing more magnificent than a self-made man, wouldn't you say, Lady Mary?'

'It is remarkable.' Lady Mary stood the same way Silas's sister Millie used to when listening to an account of a Fairclough Foundation resident's good deeds for the day. It was the slide of her eyes up and down the length of him and the appreciation and admiration dancing in them that gave her away. Silas wasn't going to have to employ flowery prose when he discussed business with her today or when their deal became final and it was simply the two of them doing what such a contract allowed them to do.

I shouldn't be thinking of that.

Still, a little flattery was never a waste.

'Lady Mary, that's a striking new watch chain you have. It's about time such a lovely timepiece had an appropriate setting.'

'I'm glad you like it since you gave it to me shortly after the investors' dinner in September. A thank-you present, I believe your valet called it.' The wry upturn of her full lips added to the chill-kissed blush heightening the apples of her cheeks. Silas bit back a laugh at having been caught out.

So that's what Tibbs purchased for her. I should have asked.

'Then I'm heartened to see it put to such good use.' Especially today.

'A very practical, and apparently memorable, gift. But I don't suppose you're here to discuss watch chains.'

'I'm here because you invited me, or should I say, told me to come.' This deepened the blush of her cheeks.

'Yes, I did. Mrs Parker, will you see what's keeping the tea?'

'At once.' Mrs Parker hustled out the door.

'Do you think it's prudent to dismiss your

chaperon?' Silas joked, amused at the older woman's alacrity in abandoning her charge.

'I don't think you'll spread any rumours about us having been alone together or make any untowards advances.'

'How very trusting of you.'

'I've been told you're a very trustworthy gentleman. Shall we?' She made for the sofa and Silas followed her precise steps, conscious that Mrs Parker had left the sliding doors open, not wishing to compromise Lady Mary's reputation too much by shutting them. He wasn't concerned about servants listening. Those in Richard's employ were discreet with Silas's and Richard's affairs, and quite free with their gossip where the doings of business partners who had more loose-lipped servants were concerned. Healthy annual wages with a great many benefits and regular tips ensured their loyalty.

'I hope I'm not keeping you from any other engagements,' Silas said as he sat down.

'My afternoon is completely free.' She spread her skirt out around her, placing a respectable amount of distance between them.

'Good, because engagement is exactly what I wish to see you about.'

'I rather suspected it would be.'

'You listen at doors, don't you?'

She didn't blush or drop her gaze from his, her confidence admirable. 'From time to time I might happen by a room in which gentlemen are discussing various matters. I can't help what I overhear and I don't pay it much mind unless it pertains to me.'

'How interesting, I have the same habit. My parents used to complain a great deal about it.' Among other of Silas's shortcomings. 'Especially since my twin sister, Millie, doesn't possess that particular inclination.'

'So listening at doors when people talk about us is the first thing we have in common.'

'Let's see what other interests we share.' He settled against the back of the sofa. 'I prefer things of a more luxurious nature, as far as my means allow. I don't like debt or puritan sensibilities.'

'Neither do I, but until recently I haven't had the ability to indulge my preferences. It's an oversight Mrs Parker and I are working to correct.'

He motioned to her dress. 'The two of you have done an excellent job of it.'

'I'm glad you approve.'

'But I think your attire is lacking in one important detail.' Silas removed a small velvet box from his coat pocket and opened it to reveal the ring inside. His heart beat hard against his ribs as he held it out, more nervous than he was when investing money in a venture. In those endeavours there was always the chance of failure, but those risks weren't as personal as this one and their success didn't impact his life in quite the same manner. It was a hell of a die to cast, but he'd done it. The rest was up to her.

She gasped at the sight of the glittering diamond ring, but made no move for it. 'You do come prepared.'

'I can't take credit for it. Tibbs, my valet, chose it. He has a much better instinct for what baubles ladies prefer than I do. I've never asked him how he came about that particular knowledge, but I think we can both guess.'

'I think we can and tell him I'm most appreciative of his tastes, and yours.' She still didn't take the ring out of the box and set it on her finger or agree to the proposal. Perhaps she was waiting for a more formal declaration although he would have thought the ring would have been enough. Apparently, it wasn't. This must be where a touch of wooing needed to come in.

He took the diamond out of the box and reached for her hand, but she gently moved it out of his reach.

Silas's grip tightened on the ring. This was not going at all how he'd imagined.

'Before we settle on anything, Mr Fairclough, we must be entirely honest with one another,' she stated the way his lawyers usually did when he was negotiating a contract.

'Honesty is always appreciated.' He didn't put the ring away, but continued to hold it where she could see it and be tempted by it and everything he was offering. She hadn't rejected him yet. If his skills of persuasion were as good as Richard claimed, she wouldn't reject him at all.

'Being a fellow countryman, you understand better than anyone how unusual it is for the unmarried daughter of an earl to live in another country under another man's care and that there must be a reason for it.' Her voice wavered with each word, but she remained steadfast in her desire to speak and he admired her courage. She was being more forthright with him than some of the businessmen he dealt with.

'But we aren't in England, are we?'

'Where we are doesn't change what happened and how it could impact any future that we wish to create for ourselves, especially with all your business dealings in England, Mr Fairclough.'

'Please, call me Silas.' He wanted to hear his name in her lilting voice, to draw her in closer to him so she couldn't refuse his offer.

'Silas, my past could impact your future and I don't want it to do that or to ever have you look at me and regret that we married.'

'I've never regretted any other investment before, there's no reason to think I'll regret you.' He cuffed her under the chin, trying to disperse the pall of seriousness that drained the light from her eyes.

'You can't say that because you don't know. You don't know what happened.' She jerked her chin away from his hand and rose and went to the fire, picking at the marble while she spoke. 'I want to be your wife, to be on your arm at balls and the theatre, to sit at the head of your table, but I don't ever want to see you turn your back on me because I'm not who and what you think I am. I endured that once before. I can't endure it again.'

The shame in her voice cut him deep because it was the same feeling that plagued him on the dark nights when he allowed himself to think back to Liverpool and the letter he'd written to his mother before he'd boarded the ship, the one that hadn't reached her until he was miles out to sea. Richard had called him brave for daring to strike out on his own to achieve his dreams. He called himself a coward for having sneaked away because he knew his mother would object. He refused to allow Mary to suffer about her past decisions the way he did.

'You won't have to endure it because I won't walk away. I know exactly who you are. You're the woman who stood beside me last night and went along with every one of my bald-faced lies and whimsical ideas, the one who sat at the head of Richard's table and flattered potential investors, the one before me at this very moment unafraid to show me her true self and not running from yet another of my crazy ideas. That's the woman I want for my wife.'

'Be serious, Silas.'

'I am being serious.' He came to stand behind her, the ring pressing the outline of itself into his palm where he clutched it. 'We've all done things we regret, Mary, failed to live up to the expectations of others, especially loved ones.'

'But what happened…'

'Unless it involves killing off rich husbands, which, given your present financial situation, suggests you're not in the habit of doing, I don't want to know about it.'

'Killing them, no, scaring them off, well… that's a different matter,' she said with a laugh half-choked with bitterness. Whoever had hurt her, he'd done a hell of a job crushing her trust. Silas would do all he could to rebuild it, the way he'd had to do for himself in the years after his father's death, the way he still worked to do.

'I don't scare easily. If I did, I wouldn't have half the success I enjoy.'

'You might have a great deal less of it if we marry and someone from England tells everyone what happened to me.'

'If they do, I'll call them out for besmirching my wife's good name.'

'You'd call a man out for telling the truth?'

'Yes, because what's done is done and there's nothing either of us can do to change it. What we decide to do from here on out is the only thing that matters, not the past.'

She straightened a porcelain figure of a shepherd kissing a shepherdess. 'But it might some day.'

'And we'll deal with it then, together as husband and wife, assuming it ever even arises at all.' He clasped her hand and slipped the ring on her finger. 'There's more to us than our pasts and our failings, and together we can help one another discover what that entails.'

Mary slid her hand out of Silas's grip and studied the ring, amazed that he still wanted her, that her past didn't matter to him. Almost everyone she'd ever known and loved had turned their backs on her and here was a near stranger offering her more comfort and forgiveness than they'd ever shown. She couldn't fathom why. Surely there was some unsullied Baltimore girl who could give him everything he sought without fear of gossip or worse. If there was, he'd chosen Mary over that unnamed woman and she should thank her lucky stars. She was hesitant to do so, afraid he and everything he was offering would be snatched from her the way it had been after Preston and then again when Ruth had died. Silas was the most tolerant gentleman she'd ever encountered and she feared it was all too good to be true. 'How can you be so understanding?'

'It'll all make sense to you when you eventually meet my family.' He twisted the gold signet ring on his pinkie finger, the air of optimism that always encircled him fading for a moment. 'I might be a success here, but coming to America, and other things, have made me quite the disappointment back home.'

'I'm so sorry.' She laid her hand on his, offering what comfort she could. Whatever mistakes he'd made, he hadn't allowed them to destroy or define him and she admired him for it as much as she'd marvelled last night at his confidence in society. For far too long she'd let her mistakes smother her, but not any more. She would strive to be more like him and look to the future instead of being dragged down by regret.

'Don't be.' He laid his hand over hers, cupping her fingers between his, the tenderness in his expression easing her fears and raising the slow rhythm of her pulse. He stood over her, the two of them so close she could see the delicate pattern in the wool weave of his brown waistcoat. His hand in hers was clean, as expected of a gentleman, but the heady scent of sandalwood shaving soap and coal dust surrounding him spoke of hard work and it called to her more than Preston's French-milled scent ever had. Mrs Parker was right, there was something very enticing about this self-made man who possessed the strength of character to succeed and the tenderness to forgive.

'What shall I be, then?' she asked, laying her hand over his.

'The happy bride-to-be.' He lifted her hand over her head and twirled her around, making her laugh in a way she hadn't done in years and breaking the seriousness that had settled between them. She was near breathless when she faced him again, the room spinning, her skirt swinging around her legs. She steadied herself in front of him and his fingers tightened around hers. She heard the catch in his breath for it matched the one in her chest. In the depths of his eyes flickered the desire running beneath this very sensible proposal, the one she'd noticed when she'd taken off her coat and he'd admired more than her watch chain, the one that had left her dizzy last night when he'd laid the cloak on her shoulders. She'd longed for him to sweep the naked skin of her shoulder with his lips as much as she craved his arms around her today. It hinted at more than a simple business proposal, but the promise of a pleasurable union. She shouldn't desire this aspect of things, it made her no better now than when she'd fallen for Preston's lies, but she couldn't help herself. Silas was not Preston.

'I promise, I will be.'

'Good.'

She held her breath, waiting for him to bend down and take her lips, but he didn't. Instead he let go of her hands, showing a restraint she wished she could better master. She took a small step back, determined to prove that she was as respectable as he believed.

'I also want you to be ostentatious in amassing your trousseau. Have Mrs Parker make appointments for you with the most fashionable merchants in Baltimore. I'll establish an account for you to draw on so you can spend accordingly.'

'I don't need it. I have my pin money from Richard to buy things.'

'And you'll keep it. It's important for a woman to have her own money so she can spend it without her husband questioning her.'

This surprised her as much as his insistence on carrying through with the proposal. Her mother had never been allowed to have her own income or even spend so much as a ha'penny on anything without her father demanding she justify the expense. Mary had fallen under the same suffocating scrutiny when she'd come of age and suddenly things were needed for her coming out. She hadn't been able to buy as much as a new fan without worrying about her father. It's why she'd fallen so easily for Preston and his tricks. A trinket here and there had been enough to tempt her into mistakes. Except Silas wasn't offering her baubles and false promises, but belief in her and a respectable marriage. 'I don't wish to take advantage of your generosity.'

'I assure you there's little generous about it. I want people to think you're spending your own money, the considerable fortune your father settled on you when you, I don't know, make up whatever story you wish about why you're here. There isn't anyone to dispute it. This is a chance to begin again, Mary, I want you to have fun with it.'

Fun wasn't how she'd ever think of her past, but the idea made her smile. She'd been all but hiding at Richard's and at a real loss for what to do next, afraid to do anything for fear her past would rise up to slap her down. Here was a gentleman, a fellow countryman who didn't care what had happened and who was offering her the chance to start over, not as some forgotten and derided lady's companion, but as the wife of a prominent businessman and member of society who would finally take her place at the head of a table as an honourable wife. It was far more than she ever could have imagined when she'd set sail from England. She would do her best to make him proud and to be the partner he desired. Even if this was not the grand love match she'd once dreamed about in London, they would be a success, she'd make sure of it.

Chapter Five

'What is all this?' Mary asked when Mrs Parker escorted her into the sitting room. It was the first week of January and, in the four weeks since Silas had proposed to Mary, the two of them had spent Christmas and New Year's Eve together at balls and dinners and private parties with various prominent members of Baltimore society. In the midst of the festivities, their time alone had been greatly curtailed, the two of them having become very much sought-after guests since word of their engagement had spread. His appearance this morning was an unexpected surprise, although they weren't likely to enjoy too many private conversations today. Silas stood in the centre of the large rug, thumbs hooked in his waistcoat pockets, beaming with pride. The masculine room had been transformed into a lady's paradise with bolts of fabric leaning against the walls, stacks of ladies' pattern books piled on the tables and Mrs Lindsey, Baltimore's leading dressmaker, waiting for Mary with a number of assistants.

'Your dress fitting, my dear fiancée.' Silas opened his arms to the room, but she noticed the slide of his gaze to the dressmaker's assistants whose jaws dropped at the news. The dressmaker's eyes practically flashed with coins as she imagined the windfall order she was about to receive.

'But I have dresses,' Mary whispered, hesitant to object and see all the beautiful fabrics packed away, especially the bolt of blue silk. She'd owned a gown that shade of blue during her Season and she'd worn it as many times as she could, much to her mother's displeasure. It had been her favourite. Of all the possessions she'd been forced to leave behind when she'd been packed off to Ruth's, that dress had been the one she'd regretted giving up the most.

'And they're fine, but a more extensive wardrobe is needed for a lady of your status. You also haven't been taking advantage of my generosity with the merchants and it's time we rectified that. I've already paid Mrs Lindsey for her time so you might as well enjoy it,' Silas whispered in reply before taking her hand and raising it between them so that the large diamond flashed in the morning light.

He drew her towards the fabric and the small fitting stool in the centre of the room, making it abundantly clear that they were putting on a show for the dressmaker and her assistants who would be certain to spread tales throughout Baltimore society about this fitting and how much was being spent on her trousseau. Mary wondered if Silas had paid them a little extra to make sure that they did tell everyone. It wouldn't surprise her, nor would it upset her. It'd be marvellous to be stared at and whispered about because she was going to be a wife instead of for uglier reasons.

Silas helped Mary up on the stool. Mrs Lindsey snatched up her measuring tape and, with her assistants trailing behind her, set to work, rattling off the many items Mary would need. Mrs Parker sat on the sofa, watching with glee and suggesting more than a few pieces to add to the list.

'In the meantime, while we're putting the

finishing touches on your new wardrobe, I have a number of dresses from unfinished orders that can be altered to suit you,' Mrs Lindsey offered and two more assistants approached Mary carrying a small selection of new gowns including a carriage dress, a tea dress and a ball gown in pale pink. Mary wanted to hop off the stool and rush to try them on, but she remained where she was. She wasn't about to fall on the clothes like a hungry dog did a piece of bread thrown in the street. She had some dignity.

'Normally, I would not suggest pre-sewn gowns for the daughter of the Earl of Ashford,' Silas drawled from where he leaned against the fireplace mantel, watching her the way the vicar used to do when Mary would help Ruth distribute gifts at Christmas to the village children. 'But I think this time we can make an exception.'

It wasn't his demeanour as the benevolent fiancé that rankled Mary, but his casually dropping her father's title. She could practically hear the assistants taking her measurements titter at the words. All they did was make her blood boil.

Mary stepped off the stool and marched up

to Silas. 'Might I have a word with my dear fiancé in private for a moment?'

She walked out of the room, wondering if Silas would follow. She hadn't meant to be cross, but there was something she must make clear to him before this engagement continued.

'You aren't happy with the dresses?' Silas asked when they stepped into Richard's empty study and Silas slid the doors closed behind him. 'You can have something else if Mrs Lindsey's creations don't suit you.'

'It isn't the dresses, it's your mentioning my father in front of people who are guaranteed to gossip.'

'That was my entire reason for allowing the connection to drop. If you hadn't interrupted me, I would have eventually mentioned my illustrious heritage as well.'

'My father has done nothing for me in the past four years. I doubt he'd even look up from cleaning his hunting guns long enough to care if he heard I was in America or had died during the crossing. He'd probably breathe a sigh of relief at my demise.' Mary's hands shook as she spoke. 'At a time when I'm enjoying myself, I don't want to hear about him and be reminded of everything he refused to do for me and won't ever do for me while everyone else is doing so much.'

'I see.'

Mary unclenched her hands as Silas nodded thoughtfully and a new fear crept over her. She'd lashed out at him when she shouldn't have. They weren't married, he could still change his mind and then all the pretty dresses, the bolts of fabrics and the dressmaker would leave. Yes, she had pin money to spend on such things, but that he'd cared enough to spend his own money on her had given the experience more meaning than if she'd hired a dressmaker. He wanted her to shine and to take pride in herself. His encouragement would end after this outburst. He'd back away and tell her that this had all been a mistake the same way Preston had done at the inn. He'd take with him the possibility and liveliness that had marked the last three weeks and leave her in the grey nothingness that she'd existed in for far too long.

Silas didn't dismiss her or demand she return the ring. Instead, he tucked his hands into his trouser pockets and nodded sagely, choosing his words carefully when he spoke. 'Don't view the mention of your father as a reminder of his callousness, but as a chance for your father, unbeknownst to him and against his will, to finally do something for you. He is lending you the cachet of his name, whether he likes it or not. No matter what happened, the fact is you are still the daughter of an earl. It's to your benefit to claim that status.'

'I hadn't thought of it that way.' All she could imagine was her father hearing of it and sending her a chastising letter demanding that she cease announcing her connection to him. More than likely the letter would be from his man of affairs. He couldn't soil his fingers by writing to the daughter he no longer loved and wanted. 'And if he objects?'

'Do it anyway to irritate him. He lost his right to object when he turned his back on you.'

A smile slowly spread across Mary's lips at the suggestion. Silas was right. Despite everything that had happened, she *was* the daughter of an earl and she'd been raised to take her place beside a respectable man, to run his home and enjoy the comforts of his name and station. It was a destiny she would finally achieve.

'Are you ready to return to your fitting, Lady

Mary?' He held out his hand to her, inviting her to join him in this the way he'd drawn the businessmen into joining his railroad venture.

'I am.' She placed her hand in his, surprised by the spark that jumped between them as if she'd touched wool on a hot and dry day. For a moment, his gaze held hers and she swallowed hard. It was nothing, only the thrill of a conspiracy, the secret they shared about themselves and the future they would create. A future. It'd been so long since she'd been able to imagine one and it made her practically float back to the sitting room as he tucked her hand in the crook of his elbow and escorted her there.

'What kind of wedding would the daughter of an earl like?' Silas asked as they crossed the entrance hall. 'Something simple in a judge's office or an elaborate church wedding with too many flowers and guests?'

The Mary who'd spent the last four years in the solitude of the country, forced to forget everything she'd been raised to do, almost said the simple affair. However, the woman who'd glowed on Silas's arm at the ball, who felt alive and excited for the first time in years, the one who'd cried over the news of her sister's wedding because it had reminded her of everything she'd lost with her stupid mistake, wanted the church, dress, flowers and guests. She wanted to be that hopeful, excited Mary again. 'The church wedding.'

'Good, because that's what I want, too. What better way to launch our union than with a grand affair?' He escorted her into the sitting room and helped her up on to the stool. 'Then I'll leave it to you and Mrs Parker to arrange the details.'

He bowed, a smile of conspiracy dancing on his lips before he took his leave, sliding the doors closed behind him.

'The first thing we need is a wedding dress,' Mrs Parker announced, 'and then, of course, some things for the wedding night.'

Mary shifted on the stool, the assistant's giggles making her stomach flutter as much as the idea of her wedding night with Silas. After Silas's proposal, she'd spent far too much time imagining what he might look like without his waistcoat than was proper or prudent, and it scared her as much as it made her toes curl. She'd been intimate with a man before and it had cost her everything. Silas hadn't wanted to hear the details, but he must have guessed the gist of it. She doubted he'd hold her lack of innocence against her, but she'd failed to carry Preston's child. What if she couldn't carry Silas's? He might forgive her past, but if her future was one of barrenness, then the patience and understanding he'd shown might wear as thin as those of her father's friends who'd waited in vain for a son. They'd eventually turned from their wives to mistresses and if this happened to her she would have to bear it with fortitude like they did, watching as the care and concern that Silas had promised her, that she craved when she was in his presence, was given to another. There was no way to know how it would be until they were married and after that there would be no going back. She wasn't about to cry off and have all the excitement and possibility encircling her vanish to a cold, dull nothingness she refused to endure ever again. She must cast her lot and, like Silas, hope for the best. With her past still hovering over her, it wasn't an easy thing to do.

'Have any letters from my family or word from England about the bank drafts arrived?'

Silas asked when Mr Hachman entered his office with the morning correspondence. Since leaving Lady Mary to the modiste yesterday, Silas had been engulfed in a flurry of work that had left him no time to enjoy a leisurely evening with his soon-to-be wife.

'No, sir, nothing.'

Silas sat at his desk, ignoring the business letters Mr Hachman laid out in neat rows in front of him. Silas had been anxiously awaiting news from his family, a little word to set his mind at ease. His being no closer to learning about what had happened to them or the bank drafts increased the guilt that had been eating at him for some time. Once again, he'd been too involved with his own life and business, both professional and personal, to see to his other duties. It was his responsibility to send money and make sure it was received. He'd failed to do so and none of the people he'd hired to do the job had managed it properly either. If he were in England he could get to the bottom of how dire the financial situation at home was, but he wasn't there, he was thousands of miles away, a choice he'd made.

'I trust the letter to Lady Alexandra with the bank note was sent?'

'They were dispatched by a special courier on the next steam ship out. If your family is dealing with some financial difficulty, the delivery should ease their situation. We'll hear something as soon as possible.'

Silas tapped the blotter. Even by steamship it would take two weeks for a letter to reach his mother, assuming the weather didn't delay it. The gulf between him and his family that he'd created when he'd left for America five years ago was widening again.

'Unfortunately, sir, there is other bad news from England. Mr Williams has grave reservations about extending the Baltimore Southern an American patent for his steam engine.' Mr Hachman laid the letter from the engine designer on top of the other correspondence. 'He's nervous about the lack of control he will have over production from so great a distance and that his designs might be stolen.'

Silas read the missive which amounted to little more than a litany of Mr Williams's concerns about stolen ideas and a lack of oversight.

'Our man in England assures me he's doing

all he can to assuage Mr Williams's fears and convince him to grant the patent,' Mr Hachman explained.

'If he's anything like our solicitor, then that isn't a comfort.' Silas stood at the window overlooking the rail yard and the large glass and steel building. The glass panes glistened in the sun, graceful and beautiful in their curving design, but the building was empty. The longer that building sat idle, the more money it cost the railway. New tracks were no good if there weren't trains to run on them.

The door to the office swung open and Richard strolled in, his cheerful smile dropping at the sight of the glum faces that greeted him. 'All not well?'

'There's some trouble in England.' Silas explained about his family and Mr Williams's reservations about the steam-engine patent. 'If Mr Williams was in America, I could wine and dine him enough to convince him to give us the exclusive patent on the engine, ease his fears and help him see the benefit in trusting us.'

'Then go to England and woo him as you would any other investor.' Richard rested his hand on the silver head of the walking stick between his legs where he sat in the chair before Silas's desk.

He should be jumping at Richard's suggestion, but something inside him recoiled at the idea of returning to England. 'I can't. There's too much to do here.'

'I can oversee things until you return. As you've said before, the Baltimore Southern is practically running itself.'

'I can't do that to you.' The responsibilities that Silas had taken over in the last few months had eased the burden on Richard and his health. He didn't wish to force him into an even earlier grave by overworking him.

'I was running businesses long before you were born.' Richard laughed before coughing into his handkerchief. 'In all seriousness, if there's a good time for you to be away, it's now. Another opportunity may not present itself for a long while. You can pursue the new engine and make sure your family is all right.'

Silas drummed his fingers on the arm of his chair. Richard was right. With the foundry contract concluded and the new engine in limbo, this was the best time to visit England. It was what he would encounter at home that made him hesitate. After all these years he'd have to finally face his mother and the cowardly way that he'd left her. As much as he was loath to endure her disapproval and criticism, this was a chance to prove to her that he wasn't shirking his responsibilities and that he wasn't a disappointment. He refused to allow his fear about what he might encounter in England, especially with his mother, deter him from doing what was best for her or the railroad. He'd never flinched from a challenge or a difficult decision before, he couldn't do so today. 'Mr Hachman, I need the fastest passage available. I don't have six weeks to waste at sea.'

'The Royal Mail Steam-Packet Company is your best choice.' What Silas hoped to do for the Baltimore Southern's passenger services in the coming years, Samuel Cunard had done with steam ships crossing the Atlantic with regular schedules and at a speed that put the old cutters plying the sea to shame. 'Their ships can make the passage in fourteen days and they run a regular schedule.'

'Then book me a cabin at once.' Silas could be in England well before the month was out and have the patent and this mess of the missing funds sorted out. While he was home, he'd also do all he could to ensure that the Foundation and his mother and sister's livelihood sat on rock solid footing. He didn't wish to worry about them like this ever again.

'Will Lady Mary be travelling with you or are you going alone?' Mr Hachman asked.

'I don't know.' Silas rose and stood behind his chair, trilling his fingers on the polished walnut back of it. If Mary came with him, they would have to alter their wedding plans. There were few women who'd welcome that but, if she did, then he'd have her to himself for two weeks. Every illicit thought that he had forced from his mind this morning rushed back to him as he imagined the two of them alone in a steamer cabin with a multitude of night and days to enjoy one another without distraction. It almost made him order Mr Hachman to purchase two passages, but he didn't. Mary knew him as a success. He didn't want her beside him when his mother slammed the door in his face or berated him for having abandoned her, destroying in seconds the carefully crafted image that he'd spent years creating. He couldn't stand to have Mary see how he'd failed in his duty to protect his family, that he'd been a weak coward who'd run away instead of telling his mother the truth, that when people needed him, he hadn't always been there.

'Sir?' Mr Hachman pressed, snapping Silas out of his thoughts. He caught Richard and Mr Hachman's questioning expressions.

'I have to speak to Lady Mary.' It would give him time to consider the issue further. She might be as loath to return to England as him and then none of this debate would matter. 'For the moment, book my passage and gather all the information you have on Mr Williams. Also, arrange for more money so I can open a trust in their name so funds are never delayed again. Is Lady Mary at home, Richard?'

'She is. Pay a call on her while Mr Hachman catches me up on company business.'

'I will.'

'Silas, I hadn't expected to see you today.' Mary was glad he was here. Whenever he was near, the darkness that had dominated so much of her life over the last few years dissipated. It scared her that in so short an amount of time she was already relying on him for something as illogical as emotions, especially those that wandered too close to affection. She'd wanted to be around Preston for the same reasons, too, and that hadn't ended so well. No, this was different and she needed to stop comparing the two men and situations. It was a good sign that she and Silas enjoyed one another's company and were companionable. It would make their marriage a real partnership.

Silas stepped into the sitting room where Mary and Mrs Parker sat perusing the latest fashions in *Godey's Lady's Book* while discussing plans for the wedding. Mary and Mrs Parker had spoken with Reverend Dr Bend at St Paul's Church yesterday afternoon and he'd given them a number of dates to choose from for the ceremony. With Silas here she could ask him which dates he preferred and once that was settled then everything else from the florist to the invitations could be arranged.

'Mary, may I speak to you alone?' Silas asked with a seriousness that had been lacking in any of their previous encounters.

He's going to cry off.

She slowly laid down her magazine, unable to control the slight tremor in her hands. Her life would not change and she would never be more than a disgraced woman. 'Of course. Mrs Parker, do you mind?'

Mrs Parker exchanged a concerned glance with Mary, making it clear she harboured the same fear about Silas. Slowly, Mrs Parker took her magazine and left.

'I'm afraid we have to make some changes to the wedding,' Silas announced the moment they were alone.

'What kind of changes?' Mary sat on the edge of the sofa cushion, doing all she could to not jump up and run off to cry. He must have finally realised that he shouldn't align himself with damaged goods. Once again a life she'd imagined was being snatched away.

'There's a problem with the English engine patent and I need to personally appeal to the holder's better business sense to overcome it. There's also some difficulties with my family that I have to attend to. I must leave for England immediately.'

'I see.' Mary flicked one of the prongs holding the diamond in her engagement ring with her fingernail. At least the reason he'd concocted for leaving her was far more noble than the one Preston had chosen. Given the stricken look on his face, he was anxious about his family's welfare, more so than her father or brother had ever been about hers. Still, here she sat, waiting for one more man who she thought cared about her to turn his back on her.

'I'm leaving on the first available steamship, but before I go, I want to know if you wish to be married by a Justice of the Peace and travel with me or remain here and have a church ceremony when I return?'

Mary almost fell off the sofa. He wasn't crying off, but offering to wed her sooner if she wanted. She thought of the beautiful wedding gown she'd ordered from the dressmaker and how she'd never get the chance to wear it to the church as she'd always dreamed, that she would lose the opportunity to have the kind of wedding that Jane had enjoyed, but if she waited for something as silly as a dress she might lose the more important aspect of a husband and the future. 'We can wed before you leave in front of the Justice of the Peace.'

'You don't mind giving up your grand church wedding?'

'I do, but I'd mind it more if I lost you to

some Englishwomen desperate for a successful America husband,' Mary offered with a forced laugh because it was no joke, but a very real concern. 'Some nobles are willing to trade a younger daughter for a little new money.'

'A little would be all they'd get from me. They have estates they can learn to better manage if they need funds. Work never hurt a man.'

'Don't say so in front of them or they'll die of apoplexy.'

'We can't have that, especially since the Fairclough Foundation relies on donations from the wives of such men.'

'The Fairclough Foundation?' Neither Richard nor Silas spoke much about Silas's past and Mary never thought this curious. She'd learned to despise hers and didn't blame others for thinking very little of theirs.

'My family runs a home for women who've fallen on hard times through various troubles. They also offer faithful servants who are too old to work but have been turned out by not-so-faithful employers a place to live. The older women help train younger women in the skills they need to earn a living for themselves and often their children.'

Mary unconsciously touched her stomach and shivered. If she hadn't lost the child in that awful inn, she and it might have found themselves in the gutter due to Preston's inability to honour his promises. Given how fast he'd abandoned her, it wasn't hard to think he might never have married her even if they'd made it to Scotland.

'My mother and father started the Fairclough Foundation after my father's beloved nanny was let go by his father without a reference and had nowhere else to turn. My father vowed never to allow something like that to happen again. Sadly, the need for such services outweighs what the Foundation can supply. I regularly send money for my mother and sisters' upkeep so the donations they receive can be used for the Foundation. They haven't received the money for some months.'

'I see.' No wonder Silas hadn't been too concerned about her background. Nothing in it could shock a man who must have seen many women with stories like hers and tended to them in their darkest moments in a way her family never would have done. She could have used sympathetic people like that in her life back then, but there'd been no one, except Ruth. 'You and your family are very generous.'

'I haven't been involved in the Foundation for many years. I greatly respect my family's work, but I don't share their passion for it, much to my late father's great disappointment.' He twisted his signet ring, regret and guilt, two feelings she knew intimately, heavy in his words.

'I'm sure he'd be proud of you if he could see everything you've accomplished.'

'No, he wouldn't be. He always looked down on men who wanted to make money. He believed it couldn't be done without others suffering. Had he lived I might have proven him wrong, but I doubt it. Now, I've let my mother and sisters down with this awful debacle. I've written to Lady Alexandra, my father's cousin, about the matter, but I've had no reply and I still don't know the full extent of the situation.'

She came to stand beside him as he'd come to her the day he'd proposed and laid a comforting hand on his shoulder, the fine wool of his coat soft against her palm. 'You'll make it right, I'm sure you will.'

* * *

Silas stared into the fire, watching the flames leap over the top of the log. He could make this financial situation right, but he couldn't correct the damage it must have done to his mother's already questionable opinion of him and his pursuits. Death had ended the possibility of making things right with his father. The old guilt that had haunted him on the crossing from Liverpool to America, the one that had pricked him every night he'd spent at Richard's working towards the kind of success his father had scorned, hit him again, but it was lighter with Mary's soft hand on his shoulder. She didn't call his guilt silly like some women had or try to dismiss it like the few men he'd dared to discuss it with in the early days, but listened with an understanding not even Richard had ever shown. She'd experienced regret and disappointment and how it could eat at a person no matter how high or low in the world they might be.

'What is it you said to me? There is more to us than our pasts and our failings, and together we can help one another find it,' Mary reminded him.

He took her hand and clasped it to his chest. She looked up at him with a tenderness to take his breath away, the firelight playing in the gold wisps of hair framing her face. He'd never had his own words used against him and he silently thanked Richard for bringing them together. He didn't want her to see the ugly rift between him and his mother or how he'd failed to live up to her expectation, but he didn't want to face that alone either. With Mary beside him as an ally, maybe he could finally find some peace with the choice he'd made. 'You may not get the wedding you want, but I promise we'll host a party to celebrate our nuptials on our return that will more than make up for your loss.'

'Our return?' Her hand went stiff in his.

'I want you to come to England with me.'

Mary forced herself to leave her hand in Silas's and not jerk it away. He was asking her to risk facing the people she'd left behind. She was no coward, having travelled to Richard in America on nothing more than Ruth's recommendation, spending six weeks at sea on the clipper in her cabin miserable with seasickness and no one to help her except the young Irish girl who she'd paid to take care of her. That girl had stepped off the boat and into the arms of her family, while Mary had gone to Richard not knowing what to expect. In the end, it had all worked out far better than she could have imagined, but she didn't want to draw upon the will and courage to face her demons again. She wanted to leave them across the sea where they could do her much less harm. 'I'd prefer to stay here and establish our home, as well as represent your interests while you're gone.'

'No, you must come. This might be my last opportunity to return to England for some time. I want you to meet my family, especially my sisters.'

'I can't risk seeing anyone I used to know and having all the old demons dragged up again.'

'I doubt you'll encounter any old acquaintances in the parts of London we'll be in, not unless your mother has a habit of patronising charitable foundations.'

'No, she does not.' Mary had once thought her mother the most loving and wonderful person in the world, until she'd discovered just how uncharitable she could be. She'd turned her back on her own daughter. Even a wedding ring wouldn't rehabilitate her in her parents' eyes and there was nothing they could do after the way they'd treated her to redeem themselves. 'Charity isn't a trait that my family is particularly familiar with.'

'Thankfully, mine are, at least where everyone besides me is concerned. They won't judge you, if that's what you're concerned about.'

Yes, she was. It was one thing to help fallen women, it was quite another to welcome one into the family. 'What about Lady Alexandra? Who knows what she's heard about me?' Or what she'd say once she learned Mary was now related to her.

'She rarely travels to London.'

'London news travels fast.'

'Given her propensity for port, she may not remember everything she's heard, especially if the story is old.'

'Stories like mine never grow old.' Time wasn't powerful enough to make society forget about a fallen woman. Preston might have been forgiven for his part in the affair, having endured little more than a few whispers and askance looks from matrons but, as Jane had unfortunately pointed out in one of her first letters to Mary, it hadn't stopped him from marrying well.

'You needn't meet her if you don't wish to, but it would mean a great deal to me for you to meet my family. Like you, I'm not entirely certain what I'll face when I get there. I don't know how dire their situation is.'

Mary traced the filigree on her watch, making the chain clink against a button on her dress. Silas's family might be suffering and he was asking for her help and support, the kind a wife pledged to give to her husband when they stood together at the altar. She couldn't allow her fear to deny him this or make her break the wedding vows before she'd even taken them. He wanted his wife, her, with him. She couldn't surrender her natural place beside him because of worries—if she did, it risked driving him away. He was a man of evidence and logic and if she presented him with too many reasons why she was not worthy to be with him, then he might change his mind and go to England with the promise of returning and then forget about her. She never wanted to be in that limbo again or to face another man deeming her unworthy of becoming his wife. She would be married and if it meant going to England and risking facing her past to do so, she would, no matter how much she wanted to be rid of England for good. 'I'll come and meet your family. I'm sure I'll love them as much as you do.'

'Thank you.' He raised her hand to his mouth, pressing his lips to the bare flesh and raising a chill along the length of her arm. She wanted to slide her hand up to his cheeks and draw him in to a kiss, to taste his gratitude as much as the longing in the firm press of his fingers against her palms, but she didn't move. She didn't wish him to think her forward or more of a tart than her past already made her. She wasn't a loose woman, but with him so close and already pledged to her, with his need for her beside him when he faced who knew what troubles, it was difficult to not slide into his arms and lay her head on his chest. 'I'll have my man arrange for the Justice of the Peace at once.'

Good. For the sooner they were joined in a proper union, the sooner she could stop holding back or worrying about her future.

Chapter Six

Mary held tight to the bouquet of flowers as she stood across from Silas, the pale pink ball gown she'd acquired from the dressmaker standing in for the magnificent cream bridal gown that awaited her return and the grand party that Silas had promised. The rotund Justice of the Peace took his place of prominence before the fireplace while he recited the marriage ceremony. Mrs Parker and Richard stood as witnesses to the proceedings, Mrs Parking weeping noisily into her handkerchief. The same efficiency that Silas employed with the Baltimore Southern had been used to organise this simple marriage ceremony. Mary had been stunned when a note had arrived informing her that it would take place the next morning for they were to set sail the day after. Thankfully, the hurried packing of her trunks and the sending over of a few of her personal items to Silas's house had kept her from thinking too much about what waited for her in England or tonight after the ceremony.

'Do you, Silas Fairclough, take Lady Mary Weddell to be your lawfully wedded wife?' The stout man with spectacles perched on the end of his round nose read from his book.

'I do.' Silas beamed at Mary, who wasn't sure if he was besotted because they were getting married or incredibly proud of the efficiency with which he'd organised the ceremony. This was the most-respected Justice of the Peace in Baltimore, Silas having insisted that if they were going to be married in such a simple fashion then he was the most fashionable gentleman to perform the ceremony. Afterwards, they would enjoy a wedding breakfast in the dining room and then the two of them would venture to the Lord Baltimore Hotel for one night together before they set sail tomorrow. Hopefully, tonight would be a great deal less fumbling, hurried and awkward than her encounters in the stable and carriage with Preston had been and far more comfortable. The grand hotel was well appointed and more pleasant than the heaven-knew-what accommodations they'd have aboard the steamship. This time she would only have to endure a voyage of fourteen days as opposed to six weeks. She didn't think she would make for a very pretty newlywed when she was green about the gills for so long.

She returned her attention to the ceremony, answering when the Justice of the Peace asked her the same questions he'd asked Silas. Before she knew it, the wedding rings were exchanged and the judge announced to everyone, including the still-weeping Mrs Parker, 'I now pronounce you man and wife. You may kiss the bride.'

Mary froze in front of Silas, not sure why she was so shocked by the idea of being kissed by her husband. As Mrs Parker had said at the ball, Mary was a woman of experience and there was nothing about this that should surprise her, but she could feel the shaking in her building when Silas stepped forward. Until this moment, she'd only enjoyed the innocent holding of hands with him and a few harmless fantasies about what this moment and a few others might be like. Now that it was real, it all seemed so much more intimate.

Don't be a silly chicken.

After what she'd done with Preston, breaking the rules of society and the church in the process, this was nothing. She was a lawfully wedded woman and not even her disapproving parents could cast a sidelong glance at her because of it. She tilted her face up to Silas, inviting his kiss.

The curls of Mary's blonde hair drawn back from her face brushed her shoulder where the dress ended to reveal the enticing curve of her shoulders and neck. He regretted their not having been able to stand in the church, in front of a marble altar surrounded by whitewashed walls shining as brightly as the diamond band he'd slipped on her finger. Silas had overlooked her the first few times they'd met. Today, he couldn't take his eyes off this woman who would be closer to him than any other woman had been before. The intensity of his reaction to her startled him, for this had all begun as a sensible business proposal and in a short time it had changed into something more. He leaned down and touched his lips to hers. They were warm and inviting, opening slightly to accept him. Silas stepped closer to Mary and pressed his fingers into her back, savouring the curve of her body against his. This was the closest they'd ever been to each other and they would become far closer tonight. The two of them were coming together as virtual strangers about to start their married life, partners in whatever new ventures were waiting for them. It thrilled him as much as the warm tenderness of her lips against his.

Mrs Parker blowing her nose into her already-damp handkerchief brought Silas back to the room and he stepped away from Mary. Together, they turned to face their two guests. Not having to hold back any longer, Mrs Parker rushed at Mary and hugged her while Richard shook Silas's hand in congratulations.

'You make a beautiful bride, Mary,' Richard said as he placed a tender kiss on each of her cheeks.

'And you make a wonderful father of the bride.'

Silas could see that she was genuinely grateful for his presence both here and in her life.

Silas was, too, but he wished his sisters and mother could have been here as well as his father. He would see his mother and sisters soon enough, assuming nothing awful had befallen them or that his mother didn't turn her back on him when he arrived on her doorstep with as little warning as when he'd left England.

'You must have a proper wedding breakfast when you return. I'll persuade Mrs Penniman or Mrs Baxter to host one,' Richard said as the footman cleared away the last of the salmon and buttered potatoes. 'We'll launch you properly into your married life.'

'And you must serve a cake with layers. I hear they are quite the fashion,' Mrs Parker added. 'The Queen of England had one at her wedding, but of course you both probably already know that.'

'A cake with layers it will be.' Silas raised his wine glass, encouraging the others to do the same. Out of the corner of his eye, he noticed Richard's hand trembling before he set down his glass and tugged his handkerchief from his coat pocket. A shocking series of deep, distressing coughs racked him until he could barely draw breath between them or remain upright. Through the gaps in his fingers the handkerchief turned bright red. The violence of the coughs made him double over and he collapsed out of his chair. Silas hurried around the table to help his friend, Mary joining him, while Mrs Parker called for Tibbs to summon the doctor.

'Don't fuss over me,' Richard gasped before another fit of coughing silenced him. He struggled for breath as he fought the spasms that racked his slender body. When the cough finally subsided, Richard lay weak and pale on the floor, each breath laboured and phlegmy. Mary cradled his head in her lap, not caring whether or not the bleeding stained her dress while she offered him what comfort she could.

'We must get him to his bedroom.' Silas motioned for a nearby footman to help him and the two men slipped their arms under Richard's and lifted him up.

It was a long and painful walk upstairs as every few feet another worrying cough racked Richard. Once they reached his room, the footman and Silas helped him into bed while Mary dabbed his sweat-soaked forehead with a damp cloth until the doctor arrived.

Silas and Mary stood together, holding hands, as they anxiously watched the doctor examine Richard. Silas worried if he set sail tomorrow morning that this might be the last time he'd ever see his friend. He didn't want it to end like this. There was too much he wished to tell him, just like with his father, to thank him for everything he'd done.

After what felt like for ever, the doctor finished his examination and gave Richard a dose of laudanum.

'What do you think?' Silas was certain he'd hear that this was the beginning of an end he had no desire to contemplate. He wanted Richard here when the Baltimore Southern launched the new engines built from the English patent and became the dominant force in the railroads in America.

'It's quite common in cases like his for patients to have coughing fits of this nature and severity.' The doctor packed up his medical bag while he spoke. His tone was low and serious, but not as morbid as the doctor who'd examined Silas's father had been. 'The laudanum should ease it for now, but in the future they will become worse.'

'But the blood?' Mary asked. Silas draped one arm around her shoulders and gave her a comforting squeeze. She leaned in to him, taking as much comfort from him as he did from her.

'Severe coughing fits can rupture vessels in the lungs. It usually looks worse than it is, but in time the severity of the fits will weaken his lungs and do more damage. When that will happen I cannot say. Consumption varies so much from patient to patient. For some it is years and for others…' He shrugged, as helpless against the progression of this awful disease as any of them. 'Either way, he'll need a great deal of rest to recover from this fit. I can recommend some nurses who can sit with him if you'd like.'

'No, I'll do it,' Mary offered. 'I tended his sister, Ruth, when she was sick. I know what to do.' Mary looked at Silas as if she expected him to demand she turn over the care of the man who meant so much of both of them to a hired stranger so the two of them could have a wedding night and leave for England. That wasn't something Silas was about to do.

'I think that's for the best.'

Mary nodded and took the chair beside the bed where she'd sat while they'd waited for the doctor. Richard slept quietly, but there was an eerie wheezing in his lungs as he breathed, as if the moment the laudanum wore off those terrible racking coughs would return.

Silas thanked the doctor and saw him out, mulling over a thousand details as he did. When he returned upstairs he met Mary in the hallway. She'd changed out of her wedding dress and into a plain black one better suited to her duties in the sickroom.

'Mrs Parker insisted I wear something more practical,' Mary said.

'This isn't how I'd imagined our wedding night happening.'

'Nor I, but I'm glad we were here when he needed us. What will you do?'

'I must make sure my family is all right, but I don't want to leave Richard like this.' He raked his finger through his hair. He couldn't leave them to suffer or to rely on the charity of others, yet he didn't want to leave Richard either. He felt damned no matter what decision he made.

Mary laid a steadying hand on his arm. 'Go to your family. I'll stay here to take care of Richard.'

'He couldn't ask for a better nurse.' He wasn't abandoning Richard, but leaving him in the best hands possible, ones that cared about him as much as he did. 'If something happens while I'm gone, it gives me great peace to know that you're with him.'

'Nothing will happen. He's sick, but he's strong. He'll get through this and be waiting to see the new plans for the engine when you return, we both will.'

He took her in his arms and held her close, the faint scent of rosewater and warmth melding together to make his head spin. He would miss their time alone together tonight and on the ship where they could truly come to know one another but, as he reminded himself, it was only being postponed, not ended. Their time together would be that much sweeter because of the wait.

'If something changes or he improves, I'll join you in England,' she offered.

Silas wasn't sure why that promise meant so much to him, but it did. If Mary left Richard's

side, it meant that all was well and the pre-
dictions Richard had made about his demise
weren't so dire. It was difficult to tell that today.
Silas ran his fingers over her gold wedding ring.
The idea that there was someone he could rely
on to take care of things when duty called him
away offered him great comfort. 'I'll return as
soon as I can.'

Mary sat beside Richard's bed reading to
him from a small book of poetry, the third one
she'd read to him in the three days since he'd
fallen ill. The maid cleared away the breakfast tray, Richard having eaten more eggs and
toast this morning than he had during the previous ones. It was a good sign, but he was
far from well. Mary had been at his bedside
almost every moment since his coughing fit,
cleaning the blood off his lips and keeping him
comfortable. Even when Mrs Parker had relieved her so she could catch a few hours of
sleep, she'd slumbered out of exhaustion instead of necessity. The desire to be near Richard the way she'd been near Ruth had forced
her out of bed. More than once the sound of
his strained breathing had carried her back to

Ruth's small cottage in England and the terror she'd experienced as Ruth's life had slipped away. Ruth had been the only safety and security Mary had known during the four years since her parents had turned their backs on her, until she'd come to America.

Mary touched her wedding ring, the gold and diamonds warm against her skin. She'd noticed the conflict in Silas's eyes in the hallway as he'd struggled to decide between seeing to his family and attending to Richard. She'd wanted to hold him here, to convince him to stay beside her out of fear that once he left he might, like Preston, realise he'd made a mistake and walk away. With the marriage unconsummated, an annulment could easily be obtained and she would be as alone again as she'd been after Ruth had passed. It was an irrational fear, but a lack of sleep and worry for Richard continued to feed it. Preston had promised to marry her and then left her at her most vulnerable. Her family had cast her out at the moment when she'd needed them to support her. It made it difficult, with Silas so far away, to maintain faith in the promise of someone she hadn't known for very long, the solid belief in him that she possessed whenever he was near.

'Missing your husband?' Richard chuckled from his bed. He sat propped up against a mound of large pillows, the white pallor of his skin replaced by a much healthier hue today.

'I'm sorry, my mind wandered. Where was I?' She tried to return to the poetry, but struggled to see the words in front of her. She'd been thinking about Silas and Richard had guessed. She wanted to speak to Richard about her fears, but she kept silent. He had too many of his own troubles to deal with to take on her unfounded ones.

'Leave it. I'm in no mood for Shakespeare this morning.'

'Should I read you the stock pages, then?'

'No, let's talk.' He settled his hands over the white sheets. 'Why are you here with me instead of on that ship with Silas?'

Mary fingered the edge of the book, turning it over in her hands to admire the fine leather tooling on the cover. 'We decided it was best if I stayed behind to look after you. It's a great comfort to Silas to have someone he trusts with you.'

'I see.' Richard drew the sash of his dressing gown through his fingers. Outside, a cart rattled by on the street. 'I hope Silas makes some peace with his family while he's home, and with himself. He's never reconciled who he is with who they wanted him to be.'

'It isn't an easy thing to reconcile.' She'd never been able to do so with her family, but she'd never been given the opportunity either.

Richard reached over and clasped her hand, his skin much colder than it should have been even with the large fire in the grate warming the room, but his grip was strong and reassuring. 'I have a feeling Silas needs you more than I do and that you need him, too.'

She was afraid to need him too much or rush to him and find out the hard way that Richard was wrong. 'When you're better I'll join him.'

'I am better.'

'Far from it.'

'I'm not exactly one foot in the grave.'

'You didn't see yourself the other morning.'

'But I see you and how much you need a friend who isn't bedridden, someone who understands you the way Silas does and can give you hope about life instead of staring death in the face.' Richard settled into the pillows and coughed. It wasn't the chest-splitting one from the wedding breakfast, but the slight clearing of his throat that didn't require a handkerchief. Mary poured him a glass of water, but he waved it away. 'It would also do him good to have someone from America with him who understands his life here and how happy it makes him so that when the old doubts rush in, the same ones that are torturing you in his absence, he can better face them.'

'What doubts?' Silas always seemed so confident, she couldn't imagine that he was ever unsure about anything the way she was.

'About who he is and what exactly he should be doing with his life.'

'He's a businessman and quite happy.'

'In the States he is, but in England with all sorts of old ghost surrounding him it won't always seem so easy.'

Mary studied the wedding ring on her finger, the diamond sparkling in the bright light of the room. The doctor had tried to insist on keeping the curtains closed, but Mary had wanted the sunlight. What Richard was asking was for her to go home and risk facing her past the way Silas was about to do. Although she'd pledged to join Silas before and been ready to board that ship with him, she would be lying if she said she hadn't been a tiny bit glad that a situation beyond her control had prevented it. She didn't want Richard sick or suffering, but she had been guiltily relieved to stay behind in the end.

'Go be with him,' Richard urged in the face of her hesitation. 'It'll give you the chance to really get to know him, to meet his family and understand the demons he's wrestling with, and maybe face a few of your own. Perhaps then your doubts will leave you and you can help him leave some of his behind, too.'

'And if his family doesn't like me or sees me as no better than some of the women they take in?' He might have said they were charitable, but she had no desire to prod the limits of his proclamation or his family's good graces. 'What if I have to face my own family?'

'I'm not saying London won't be without its difficulties, but facing your fears instead of hiding from them might make them less formidable.'

Or it might remind her exactly why it was she was in Baltimore. She was creating a life here and while Richard's suggestion appealed to her rational self, the woman in her who'd ridden away from Foxcomb Hall with tears streaming down her face wanted to leave it all behind. 'What about you? Silas is counting on me to care for you.'

'There are plenty of people to take care of me, Mrs Parker specially, and I don't plan to expire quite yet. Go to England and be with your husband. Don't let fear of what might happen stop you from enjoying what is happening. You're a newlywed and should enjoy this time with your husband.'

Mary gripped the leather cover of the poetry book so hard the tooling imprinted on her fingertips. Richard was right. She was so occupied with worrying about what might be that she wasn't enjoying what was. She was a respectable Baltimore wife with a different future ahead of her than the one she'd spent the last few years imagining. Even if going to England meant running the risk of facing everything she'd left behind, it was a gamble she must take if she wanted to seal in earnest the contract that she and Silas had entered into. She must go to England.

Chapter Seven

Mary gratefully stepped off the gangplank and on to the dry land of England. This crossing had not been as bad as the one she'd endured to get to America, but it'd been as lonely. Mrs Parker had stayed behind in Baltimore, leaving it to the band on Mary's finger and the change in her last name to shield her from any untoward talk about a woman travelling alone. If anyone had questioned it, they'd said nothing, the ship's staff catering to her because of her connection to Silas. She'd enjoyed the respect being married had conferred on her and hoped it remained with her while she was in England. She would need it if she encountered her family, who were sure to be anything but bolstering of her no matter what her position.

No, I must not think about that. I must concentrate on reaching Silas.

Mary looked at the mass of people and things on the dock surrounding her, overwhelmed by what to do next. She'd left on a Cunard steamer the day after her conversation with Richard, his man of affairs having been kind enough to arrange the passage for her while she and Mrs Parker had decided which of the new clothes would come with her in the steamer trunk. The old Mary had wanted to bring only the plainest items while Mrs Parker had threatened to burn them if she tried to pack them.

'You are the wife of a successful businessman, how you dress reflects on him so you must look your best,' Mrs Parker had insisted with her usual wisdom. 'I'm sure the daughter of an earl knows how to do that.'

She did, at least she had at one time, so when she'd dressed this morning with the help of a young woman in steerage who'd been glad to accept better accommodations and some wages to serve as Mary's lady's maid aboard ship for the two-week passage, she'd chosen a fine travelling dress of deep blue cotton and a smart hat. The young woman had since said goodbye to Mary, throwing herself into the arms of her waiting family who'd cried at the reunion while Mary stood alone with her new trunks and dresses watching them. There was no one here to greet her.

'Mary?' Silas's voice broke through the indistinct chatter of the crowd and the clatter of cargo being loaded and unloaded.

'Silas? Why aren't you in London?' His ship had left four days before hers.

'We ran into a storm off the coast of Nova Scotia and we were delayed for four days. We just pulled in this morning.' He waved his hat at the *Britannia* moored beside her ship. 'What are you doing here? Why aren't you with Richard in Baltimore?'

She twisted the leather strap of her small valise, bracing herself for his reaction when she told him. She didn't relish him chiding her for abandoning their sick friend or for him to think that she'd chased after a man like she'd done four years ago. Except this man was her husband. She had every right to be with him. Mary took a bracing breath of the salty air mixed with the tangy scent of Silas's bergamot cologne. 'He's doing much better since you left, so much so that he insisted I join you. He practically packed me on to the steamer himself. He said you needed me more than he did.'

'He said that?' Silas rubbed his chin with his finger and thumb, staring down at the scarred wharf boards while he pondered her words. Mary shifted on her feet, waiting for him to admonish her the way her father used to do whenever she'd dirtied a dress as a child or broken something in the house while she'd played.

She unclenched her grip on her valise when Silas finally looked up at her with the smile she was used to seeing. 'If Richard insisted you come, and made the arrangements for you to join me, then I have to trust that he is well. I'm glad you're here.'

'Are you?' She shouldn't be so thrilled about his admission, but she was.

'Very much so.' He offered her his arm. 'Come, let's catch our train to London.'

Tibbs, in his usual efficient manner, saw to the transportation of their things to the Grand Junction Railway station and the train that would take them to Birmingham. From there, they would pick up the London and Birmingham Railway and make their way to London. The hustle to get something to eat and then board the train was not enough to stop Silas from thinking over the comment Mary had made about Richard. Richard had sent her here because he felt that Silas needed her. It wasn't like Silas to question Richard's reasons. He wouldn't enjoy half the success he did if he had, but this time he wondered. Other than the chance to meet his family, Silas couldn't imagine what about this trip and him would create a need so large that it required Richard to send Mary across the Atlantic alone, but it no longer mattered. She was here and they were together and they would begin their married life. It wasn't the magnificent start in Baltimore that he'd imagined, but it was better than nothing.

It was a long exhausting day by the time they reached Birmingham. If they decided to continue on to London it would be very late when they arrived, exhausted and hungry, and with no one at his family's home expecting them. He didn't want to wake his mother and sisters in the middle of the night or arrive in darkness to find the Foundation shuttered because of debt and he left with no idea where they had gone.

'We'll stay here tonight and continue on to London in the morning. It'll be good to sleep in a proper bed and have a real meal before we face tomorrow,' Silas announced as they stood on the platform while people pushed past them to exit and enter the train. As much as Silas wanted to find out what was going on, he'd be better able to deal with it rested and in the light of day. He could tell from the darkness beneath Mary's eyes and the way her shoulders drooped that she needed the rest. 'Does this suit you?'

'It does.'

'Good. Tibbs, please see to our things. Mary and I will go to the hotel and secure our rooms.'

'Yes, Mr Fairclough.' The valet wove off into the crowd to attend to their luggage and the tickets for tomorrow's train to London.

Silas escorted Mary through the glass and iron train depot, almost ashamed at how much everything he saw excited him the way it had when he'd first arrived in Liverpool. 'The Baltimore Southern must design stations like this, a testament to efficiency, and introduce the standardised ticketing we saw in Liverpool and I'm sure they have here. When we reach London, I'll send a letter to Mr Hachman to set up meetings with our New England and Southern contacts about getting them on board with the idea. It would make travel for passengers a great deal easier than the mishmash of ticketing we have now.'

Mary listened to Silas's rush of ideas as much here as she had on the train, enchanted by his energy. Even after two weeks at sea and the delay, he could still paint a picture of a future that she could believe in and wanted to see.

He escorted her down the platform and out of the station to the adjacent Queen's Hotel. She did her best to let his good nature infect her despite the weight sitting hard on her chest. It wasn't simply the prospect of facing his family tomorrow that made her tense, but what would most likely happen tonight. Alone together, the natural progression of their marriage would finally take place. She should welcome this intimate exchange since it would cement the legitimacy of their union instead of leaving it in unconsummated limbo, but she was familiar with what happened between a man and a woman in the dark and the consequences that could arise because of it. Those consequences had forced her and Preston towards Gretna Green and when she'd lost the child, it had given him the excuse he'd needed to leave her. She had no idea how Silas would react if a child came of tonight or any night. She hoped he would welcome it as easily as he had her into his life.

It didn't take long for them to reach the Queen's Hotel, a tall, square building in the Italianate style that towered over the lower station. While Silas secured rooms for the night, Mary waited on one of the comfortable sofas in the lobby, grateful to be seated on something that wasn't moving.

'Good news. Tibbs will have his own room. After being cooped up with me for the last two weeks, I'm sure he'd like a little breathing space and us a little privacy.'

'That will be nice.' Mary was somewhat disappointed that he was getting two rooms. If necessity had forced Tibbs into an adjoining room, then what was likely to happen tonight might be postponed until London. Of course, this alternate plan wasn't ideal either. What was sure to pass between them was not something she wished to try for the first time under the listening ears of Silas's mothers and sisters.

Silas dangled the small key attached to a leather tag between them. 'Shall we go up or would you prefer to eat something? There's a small restaurant off the lobby.'

'Let's go to our room. We can always have something sent up later.' She was too anxious about being alone with him to even think about forcing down food.

Whatever Silas's thoughts on the matter, he kept them to himself as he escorted her through the hotel and up to their room, his steady stream of ideas and thoughts fading into a quietness that was unlike him. She hoped it wasn't regret making him a touch more morose. There was no reason to believe it was, but she couldn't help herself. The past had taught her to doubt so many things.

They entered the small room and he closed the door behind them. It was simple, with only a wash stand, a bed and a turned wood chair to take up the narrow space. Silas and Mary only had their valises. The rest of their things had been left behind at the station for tomorrow's train. A small wrought-iron stove in the corner offered a welcome dose of heat. There was no getting away from one another in here just as there'd been no place to get away from Preston in that small inn on the way to Gretna Green, nowhere she could go to clean up the mess once everything had started. Instead, she'd lain there in pain with Preston standing at the foot of the bed scowling at her in disgust before he'd walked away.

'Shall I help you undress?' Silas asked. There was no lecherous look in his eyes, no sneering desire in his words the way there'd been in Preston's in the stables, but there was no mistaking the invitation. Mary didn't move, unsure what to do. She could simply turn around and ask him to unbutton her dress and allow things to continue as they would, aware that this time everything they did was allowed and sanctioned by society.

'Mary?' Silas pressed, sensing her hesitation as much as she did his eagerness to proceed.

'I'm sorry, it's been some time since I was last in a situation like this.' She opened her hands to the room, feeling more as if she was flailing than anything else. How dirty that sentence made her sound, as if she was not good enough for a man like Silas. She twisted her hands in front of her, waiting for him to come to that realisation, too, to turn and leave her untouched, to send another letter to his man of affairs about getting him out of this mistake. 'I'm sorry, I didn't mean to sound like a wanton woman.'

She should keep her mouth shut and stop making it worse, but she couldn't.

'I'm not averse to a wanton wife.' Silas set his hat on the chair and slipped out of his overcoat and jacket to reveal the waistcoat and white shirt underneath. He dressed well, but there was an ease to his attire, as if he simply purchased clothes, not fussed and fretted over them the way that Preston used to do. Still Mary could not turn around to reveal the buttons running down the length of her dress or allow him to undo them one by one and escort her to their wedding-night bed. He had to know the truth, to hear everything before it was too

late. She never wanted him to feel trapped the
way Preston had and have it eat at him until he
wanted nothing more to do with her.

'There were repercussions from my last...'
Mary stuttered, bracing herself for the glare
her brother and father had fixed on her or for
Silas to hang his head in disappointment the
way her mother had when she'd realised that
her daughter was not the Mary who'd left the
house days before and that she would never be
that woman again.

'What happened to the child?' There was no
accusation in his voice as there had been with
her father, simply a desire to know.

'In the end there was no child. He walked
away when it was clear there was nothing holding him to me any more.' Mary twisted the
wedding band on her finger, waiting for Silas
to put his coat back on and tell her that this
had all been a mistake. 'I was young and stupid and I've paid the price many times over.'

'As I told you in Baltimore, it's the past and
it doesn't matter to me.'

'But how can it not matter to you? The people who should have loved me the most will-
ingly cast me aside because of what happened.'

The words slipped out before she could stop them, the way her pleas for Preston to stay beside her had followed him out of the room.

Silas laid his hands on her upper arms, the weight of his touch soothing and warm and unnerving all at once. Despite what she'd revealed he was coming closer instead of running away and it frightened her. Their marriage was little more than a business transaction, yet she felt more intimate and vulnerable with him than she ever had with Preston. 'This is your second chance, Mary. Don't be afraid of it, but embrace it. Not everyone gets one of these.'

The understanding in his words touched her, but she still couldn't believe that somehow, especially while they were in England, her past wouldn't reach out to strangle them both. Until that day, which she prayed would never come, she couldn't let fear guide her. She had to join with him fully and believe that he would honour the promises that he'd made to her before the Justice of the Peace, to think as he did that this was her second chance and that she could make something of it and her time with him.

Mary slowly turned around. 'Please, help me off with my dress.'

Without a word, Silas began to undo the buttons. Mary took a deep breath as he worked each ivory one through the eyelets, the bodice along her shoulders and over her breasts loosening with each movement of his fingers. When at last she felt the fabric gape open, Silas took hold of the garment and slid it down her body to crumple on the floor at her feet. His warm breath caressed the back of the bare skin above her stocking as he held the dress for her to step out of it.

She turned to face him and he laid the dress over the turned wood chair, never taking his eyes off her. She stood before him in her corset and chemise, facing him without shame. With deft fingers he unbuttoned his waistcoat and tossed it aside, then reached up to pull his shirt over his shoulders, revealing a wide expanse of chest tapering to a narrow waist covered by his trousers. His chest was solid and firm, the body of a man of action and energy and vision. Mary reached out to touch it, wanting this same spirit and possibility for herself.

The cool air of the room hit Silas's bare skin as sharply as Mary's gentle touch. It was cautious but admiring, giving her an innocence that life had stolen from her. He didn't take her hand to stop her, but stood still while she traced the line of his shoulder and the bend of his arms. He watched her the entire time, the sight of her curving waist and hips hugged by the silk and cotton of her undergarments made her new dresses pale in comparison to her natural beauty.

The heat of her touch began to singe and he wrapped his arms around her waist to lean forward and capture her lips, free to kiss her for as long as he wished tonight. With light hands she rested her fingers on his chest, moulding against him to accept his embrace and him. With his fingers, he began to undo her stays, pulling the long laces through the eyelets as his tongue caressed her lips. She opened her mouth to accept him, wrapping her arm around his neck while he continued to work the garment loose. Within moments, the whisper of the laces through the eyelets ended and the stays slipped away to join the dress on the chair beside them. He broke from their kiss to take hold of the chemise and draw it over her head. She didn't resist, but raised her arms so that he could free the cotton from her body. He let out a long appreciative breath at the sight of her firm breasts above a flat stomach and rounded hips, the hint of blush colouring her creamy skin making him want to rush forward. Instead he held back, undoing his trousers and pushing them down over his hips to reveal his full desire for her. She didn't shy away from the sight of him, nor did she apply any artful glances or come-hither looks the way the women he sometimes dallied with in Baltimore did. She wasn't unfamiliar with a man's attentions, but she wasn't cunningly coy with them either, simply honest and open in her reactions.

He picked her up, her body soft and supple against his as he carried her to the bed. He flung back the coverlet and laid her on the soft sheets before stretching out beside her to caress her full breasts before tracing a tender line across her stomach, over her hips and down her thighs. With his fingers he untied the garters holding up her stockings and pushed the silk netting over one curving calf and then the other, the thin material, still warm with her heat, caressing his palm before he dropped them to the floor.

Stretched out beside him, she pressed herself against him, her breasts firm against his chest, her stomach warm against his member. She didn't lie passively waiting for him to lead her, but drank in his caresses, delighting in his touch and his attention as much as he did her presence. When he'd seen her on the dock in Liverpool when she should have been thousands of miles away, he'd been as excited as he'd been startled. The long nights aboard the ship, especially when the storm had delayed them, had increased his anxiety over his family. There'd been no one to share his worries with except Tibbs, who'd listened with a servant's deference, unable to truly understand Silas's fears. Mary, despite the short time they'd known one another, understood him in a way that no one had before. That, more than the feel of her body beneath his as he slid on top of her and she welcomed him, increased the connection that had been growing steadily between them ever since the Christmastime Ball. Never had he felt so close to someone in so short an amount of time, and while this in many ways made him wish to hold back, he didn't, deepening the bond between them more than the Justice of the Peace ever could have.

Mary clung to Silas as the two of them became one, his caresses slow and leading, not demanding and hurried. This was a true joining of their bodies and their lives, not the slackening of lust or the thrill of something forbidden. Shame played no part in her eagerness to surrender to him. What they were doing wasn't wrong and she followed his gentle movements, giving herself to him completely. The small fear of what might come of this lovemaking played in the back of her mind, but the slow and easy way he drove them both towards their pleasure pushed it away. Whatever came was a concern for another day, she was with Silas here in the present and as they cried out together she clung to him, not wanting to be anywhere else.

Silas lay with Mary in the crook of his arm. The coals in the stove burned orange from behind the wrought-iron grate, the hustling sounds of the hotel outside their door having settled into the quiet of night. They would have to make an early start of it and still Silas couldn't close his eyes and give in to the exhaustion making his muscles ache. There was too much on his mind, there had been since he'd boarded the ship in Baltimore. He shouldn't trouble Mary with it, but as he stared up at the small cracks in the plaster ceiling that seemed to deepen with the increasing shadows he couldn't keep silent.

'I never should've allowed it to get to this point. I was so busy with the foundry, I left it to others to manage the accounts and they failed. I failed my family.' *Again.* His father would be disappointed at Silas coming home only when there was a problem instead of having been there all along.

'You didn't fail. It simply happened and you're here to fix it.' Mary turned over on her stomach and rested her hands on his chest. The pins from her hair had come loose and her curls draped over her bare shoulders. 'The distance can be a comfort sometimes, but it can also create problems by delaying letters from loved ones and such.'

Distance. He'd placed a great deal of it between himself and the Foundation years ago and he'd struggled to close it over the last two weeks. Tonight, it felt even wider than before. 'Sometimes I regret going to America, of leaving them behind instead of taking over the way my father hoped I would.'

'But what would you have gained if you'd stayed here? You'd have made others happy while you were miserable. You would have been struggling instead of earning a living and having money to send to your sisters. They're able to do the work they do because of your work in America. That never would have happened if you hadn't left.'

'Writing a cheque isn't enough, I've seen the great men and their wives do that for the Foundation, handing money out because that's the easiest way to clear your conscience, but it doesn't clear your conscience. My father died believing that I'd be there to take his place, to carry on his work, but I couldn't do it. It wasn't the life I wanted, struggling to pay bills, relying on others to survive, never sure if there would be enough money for clothes and food, much less the women in need. During the few Christmases we spent at Lady Alexandra's country house, I used to pretend that all her fine things and the servants and the grand rooms were mine. I wanted them more than my stark bedroom and the darkness, troubles and cruelty of London. My father tried to shame that desire out of me, but he couldn't. He was afraid my need for success would corrupt me the way it had my grandfather. He couldn't see past his fears to realise that I was nothing like the earl.' Silas's grandfather had built his wealth off the slave trade and his father had spent his life trying to atone for sins he hadn't committed. What was Silas trying to atone for?

'There's nothing wrong with wanting nice things, especially when you've gained them through your own hard work.'

'My father used to say it was off the sweat of other's labours.'

'Labourers who wouldn't have work if it wasn't for you, who wouldn't be able to feed their families or provide for those they love. You share your prosperity instead of clinging to it like some miser the way my father used to do. He had the grand house and the income, but he never gave a servant more wages than he had to or took care of the sick and elderly ones without grumbling or finding some way to foist them on to the parish poor relief. It takes men of vision who are willing to risk everything they have and their futures to create work for others. There's great value in that.'

In America, in his machine shop surrounded by workers and possibilities, it was easy to see that she was right. In the darkness of an English night it was much more difficult. He hugged Mary tighter and pressed a tender kiss to her temple, thankful for her presence and her reassurances. In all the years of his life, there'd been few people who'd ever really believed in the value of his dreams. It wasn't until he'd met Richard and saw his plans for the railroad, the innovations and schematics, that something more than dreams had truly resonated with Silas. Everything he'd done with Richard had been exciting and for the first time he'd made plans instead of blindly following the plans of others. That life was thousands of miles away. Now he'd have to face up to it and the mistakes he'd left behind. 'It's time to sleep. We have a long day tomorrow.'

Mary didn't argue, but snuggled down beside him, her breathing becoming slow and steady as she drifted off to sleep. Silas continued to stare at the ceiling and the deepening shadows in the cracks. He was a liar. He'd told Mary their pasts didn't matter and couldn't bother them, and hers didn't, not to him, but his did. He hadn't shared with Mary how he'd left for America without telling his mother, sending her a letter with his poor explanations for why he'd left. He'd apologised in that letter and many others to his mother for his decisions. He had yet to discover if he had ever been forgiven.

Chapter Eight

'You can shift closer to me. I won't bite,' Silas teased.

Mary sat tucked in the corner of the hired carriage conveying them from Euston Station where the Grand Junction Railway had deposited them after carrying them to London from Birmingham. She didn't move, not even at Silas's invitation. If Silas experienced any of the twist of emotions surrounding her, then she hoped her presence was as much a comfort to him as his was to her. 'I never thought I'd be back in London again.'

'Life is strange like that sometimes, but there's no reason to hide from it.' He reached across the squabs and tugged her into the seat beside him.

'I don't want to be seen, although I doubt my

parents would dare show their faces in town before the Season begins. My father wouldn't risk being here when it isn't fashionable, but I don't wish to take a chance.' Her father's reputation had been the only thing besides his wealth that had mattered to him. If she'd been more careful with hers, she wouldn't have to cower in the shadow of a carriage as they passed Pall Mall and St James's Park and everything outside of the rig would have stayed as the backdrop to her life. Then again, if her father's most pressing concerns had been her, she never would have met Silas, Ruth and Richard. All of them had shown her what true care and concern really were.

She pressed against Silas, enjoying his firm thigh next to hers in the tight confines of the hired carriage. 'This was all so familiar to me once, a part of every year when we came to town. Now, it means nothing to me except what might have been.'

'I know what you mean. After my father died, I used to sneak out of the house and visit the London and Greenwich Railway construction sites, especially the one near London Bridge. The railway used to run sample lines of the steam engines while they were building them to give people an idea of what was possible and I would watch those simple engines for hours. Mother hated my going there, especially on the days I was so enraptured I'd forget to run some errand she'd assigned me, but I was fascinated. When I left the Foundation to take a position in the railway office, my mother nearly disowned me. Of course, my sneaking off to do it and not telling anyone where I was for a number of days didn't exactly quell her anxiety.' He tapped the tip of his walking stick thoughtfully against the rough floor, then flashed a beguiling smile, but there was no missing the pain lying beneath it. He might make light of what had happened between him and his mother, but it still troubled him.

'I imagine the money you brought in eased some of her concerns.'

'I'm not sure it did.' He glanced out the window as the carriage left St James's Park and ventured into Westminster. 'She accepted my ambition more out of necessity than anything else. Someone had to work and it couldn't be my sisters. She's the one who arranged for my position with Jasper and King Enterprises in Liverpool. Thankfully, my twin sister, Millie, could always be counted on to do what was expected of her. My mother only had to be disappointed in one of her offspring. When I left for Liverpool, I vowed that some day I'd be able to support them completely while doing what I have always dreamed of doing. Until I found out my money wasn't reaching them, I thought I'd kept my promise.'

'You did and you're coming here to make sure they're all right will mean a great deal to them.'

'I hope so.' It was the first time Silas had ever been so apprehensive and it bothered her. If someone as optimistic as him held doubts, what hope did she have for overcoming hers? Everyone lost faith in themselves at some time or another. Only most people hid it well. She was glad he wasn't hiding his from hers. She wanted to be the person he turned to when he needed support, the way she was certain she could turn to him.

They passed beneath the shadow of the Gothic towers of Westminster Abbey, its circled stained-glass window dark from the lack

of light behind it. The streets leading off the
main one were a twisting maze of poverty
and need in the shadow of the historic Abbey.
Mary was willing to sit up closer to the window here and look out at the old building as
they passed it. This wasn't a part of London
where she or any of her family members were
likely to venture. If they'd ever thought of dis-
pensing charity, it would have been through
an agent, preventing them from touching the
poor who lined the streets in this questionable
part of town. The voices of the people calling out to one another were tinged with Irish
and lower-class English accents, workers and
women running errands or selling things in the
street surrounding them. Some of the people
paused in their business to watch the coach
pass by, but the rest paid them no mind, too
busy with trying to eke out a meagre living to
worry about anyone but themselves and their
business.

The carriage turned on to Howick Place
where the street became more respectable although not out of range of the stench of the
slums that were far closer than Mary imagined many of the inhabitants here would like.

The carriage came to a stop in front of a solid red-brick building. Silas handed Mary out of the carriage and for a moment she felt more like the women coming here for refuge than she did Silas's wife. In London, even with Silas's hand in hers, it was difficult to forget her past. It was practically choking her.

'As the daughter of an earl, I imagine you've never been this deep into London,' Silas teased, escorting her up the small walk. Behind them, Tibbs worked with the driver to unload their things.

'The disgraced daughter of an earl,' Mary muttered. This was the first test of whether or not Silas's assurances that her past would not matter to them would prove to be true. It was hard to imagine that his mother wouldn't sneer down her nose at Mary for sullying her son.

'The daughter of an earl and the wife of a prosperous Baltimore businessman who happens to be the grandson of an earl.' Silas slipped two fingers under her chin and raised it up. 'Never forget either of those things, no matter what people tell you. You are someone worthy of their respect, mine and your own.'

His words gave her a measure of confidence

even if she didn't entirely believe them. It was time to stop courting troubles with her worries and face whatever waited for her. As Richard had said, none of her fears might ever come to pass. 'Yes, you're right.'

She marched up the walk, took hold of the dull brass door knocker and banged it hard against the strike plate. Silas joined her, sliding her a sideway impressed smile before the click of the lock made them both face forward.

'Silas! I can't believe it's you. Mother, Silas is here!' A young woman with Silas's eyes encircled by glasses cried when she opened the door before throwing herself into his arms to greet him with squeals and hugs. Then she stepped back, admiring his fine suit and sliding the gold watch out of the pocket by its chain. 'Look at you. If I didn't know you, I'd think you one of those titled men who drive their carriages in Rotten Row during the fashionable hour.'

'What do you know of Rotten Row and the fashionable hour?' Silas shot back, picking the young woman up by her waist and swinging her around to make her laugh. It delighted Mary to see and saddened her at the same time.

Her family would never give her this warm a welcome if she ever turned up unannounced on their doorstep. They would slam the oak doors in her face. Even if she hadn't been cast out, no husband, not even one with an estate and lineages more ancient than hers, was ever likely to get such an effusive greeting from either of Mary's parents or her siblings. Simple nods of approval would be all they could expect, even from Jane who would be forced by their father to restrain herself. It was a joy to see not all families were so stingy with their affection.

'You aren't the only one who's risen in the world.' Lottie held out her ring finger to Silas when he set her down, revealing the wedding band adorning it. 'Jasper King and I are married.'

'You and Jasper?' Silas marvelled at the ring on Lottie's finger, and the changes that the years since he'd last seen her had wrought. Gone was the childish younger sister. She was replaced by a grown woman who wore her curly hair up, the wildness of it tamed by the hand of a lady's maid and the help of fine tortoiseshell combs. The shapeless dress that used to hang on her slender little form had been replaced by a more fashionable gown that revealed the loss of her childish angles and gangling limbs to those of a woman old enough to be a wife and possibly a mother. That it should be Jasper who'd caught Lottie's heart amazed him. While Silas admired and respected Jasper, he thought him a touch too serious for Lottie's more mercurial personality, but perhaps this was why they'd been drawn to one another. He could imagine Lottie softening Jasper's tough edges while Jasper helped temper Lottie's impulsiveness. 'Why didn't one of you write and tell me the good news?'

'I did, we all did, except Mother, of course, you know how she is, but you never wrote back. We thought something might have happened until we received your letter at Christmas. It was the best present ever until this moment.'

Silas frowned, not sure which troubled him most, that his letters had never reached them or that his mother, even when there was a possibility that something was wrong with him, hadn't sent a letter. It set him on edge about meeting her again. Clearly, she hadn't forgiven him for sneaking away from England. 'I heard from my English agent that you might be in financial straits.'

Lottie's smile faltered, but in true Lottie fashion her worry didn't last long. 'We aren't any more. My marriage took so much worry off Mother's shoulders and Jasper has been no end of help to us when your money stopped coming and while we waited to hear from you.'

Silas tightened his grip on his walking stick. He was glad there'd been others to keep his family from ruin when he wasn't here to do so, but it irked him to think another man had been forced to step in and take care of them the way his father had expected him to do, the way any dutiful son should have gladly done.

'With you here, it'll be like old times with all of us together, the house full of noise and people and all our plans, perhaps even with little children soon.' She turned to Mary, eyeing her with an eagerness that made Mary step back before Silas wrapped one arm around her waist and drew her forward. 'Lottie, allow me to introduce my wife, Lady Mary. Mary, this is my younger sister, Lottie.'

'You're married and to a lady of all people. It's wonderful to meet you, Mary.'

Lottie threw her arms around Mary who stood in the grip of her hug, overwhelmed and awed by the young woman's exuberant welcome. 'Mother and Millie are going to be amazed when they find out you're here.'

Mary didn't share the girl's certainty as she glanced over Lottie's shoulder at the empty entrance hallway, waiting for Mrs Fairclough to appear and throw her out of the house.

No, stop being so afraid.

Mary hugged Lottie back with genuine appreciation of her acceptance, trying to do what Richard had said and live with things as they were instead of worrying about what might be. For the moment Silas's sister accepted her and she would enjoy it.

'Of all the times for your letters to go astray,' Lottie said when she finally let go of Mary.

'You wouldn't have heard of it through the post,' Silas said. 'We wed before we left, I didn't have time to write of the good news.'

'Then I'm glad you could tell me in person.' Lottie waved for Silas and Mary to follow her into the front sitting room. 'I don't know where Mother has gone off to, probably the Foundation, but she should be back soon. Sally, please bring in a tea,' she instructed the young maid before Lottie dropped into a chintz chair by the window. 'We all thought something had happened to you. Mother said we shouldn't worry because if something had happened then Mr Jackson would send word, but when we hadn't heard from you or received your money we couldn't help but worry.'

'I'll get to the bottom of those missing letters and the missing bank drafts, and so many other things while I'm here.' Silas set his hat and stick down and sat on the sofa beside Mary.

The gathering was cosy and warm even while Mary waited on the edge of the cushion for Silas's mother to appear. Mary hoped the welcome continued when Mrs Fairclough did arrive for she longed to revel in this comfort for as long as possible. As a child and even a young woman, she'd never experienced a sitting room this inviting until she'd lived with Ruth and Richard. It was the kind of home she longed to create with Silas in Baltimore.

Tibbs passed by in the hallway, the driver with their bags following behind him as Sally led them to Silas's room upstairs.

'A valet, too. Silas, what will you amaze us with next?' Lottie teased. 'The best part is you will both be here for Millie and Cassius's wedding ball.'

'Millie is married, too?' Silas gaped. While he'd been in America his sisters had grown up. Their lives had changed and he hadn't been here to witness it. Instead, all he'd been able to see was his ambitions for his railroad. He should have been here for the weddings, stood in his father's place to give his sisters away, especially now with travel between England and America so much easier. Instead, it'd fallen to other men to act in his place. He could only imagine what his father would have said if he'd been here and what his mother must think. 'Who's the lucky man? Someone else I know?'

'You won't believe it. Millie married the Marquess of Falconmore. It was all very hurried and almost a scandal when rumours about Millie and Lord Falconmore spending the night alone together in a gardener's house began to circulate in the village near Lady Alexandra's. It turns out the gardener was Lord Falconmore himself.'

'What was a marquess doing in a gardener's house?' Silas couldn't believe that Millie, who'd seen enough heartache from the women of the Foundation to know better, had involved herself in an illicit affair, especially with a man of such high rank.

'He was avoiding his cousin's widow who had her eye on him. Except it was Millie who landed him first, but don't worry, you won't have to call out Lord Falconmore to defend Millie's honour. He did the honourable thing, not that he did it against his will. When you see them together you'll know they're in love.'

'Then I'm glad I'm here to meet the new Marchioness.' It didn't seem possible, but Silas was already thinking of ways he could invite Millie and her illustrious husband to America, to have them visit his railroad and make a show of them to Baltimore society and his investors. Mary would know how to fête such a man. Silas turned to her to say something about it and caught the look of near panic on her face before she concealed it with a forced smile. He wondered what about the mention of Millie's titled husband had frightened her. He couldn't have been the one who'd caused her trouble, could he? He doubted his sensible sister would marry a man with a rakish past that included ruining a woman. He'd speak to Mary about it later. 'Do we all have to bow to Millie now?'

'She'll take precedence at the table along with her husband, but we won't have to address either of them as Your Grace,' Mary answered as if she were being questioned by her governess.

Lottie gave Silas a strange, questioning look.

'Mary is the Earl of Ashford's eldest daughter,' he stated simply, but it wasn't enough to stop Lottie from going wide eyed at the announcement.

She slapped him on the lapel. 'Silas, you never cease to surprise any of us.'

'Indeed, he doesn't,' Jasper King concurred as he entered the room, limping with each step. The remnants of his old injury didn't slow him much, though, as he moved with surety and purpose towards Silas who rose to shake his mentor's hand.

'Jasper, it's great to see you. Congratulations on your marriage.'

'Thank you.' Jasper was taller than Silas and more slender with black hair and brown eyes that shone with his good humour and the excitement of seeing his former apprentice again. 'I've been following the progress of the Baltimore Southern Railroad. If I'd have had any sense when you were in Liverpool, I would've listened to all your ideas about the railways and we'd have you instead of the Yanks.'

Silas introduced Jasper to Mary. 'This is the man who recommended me to Richard. We owe him everything.'

'Then I'm even more grateful to you than my husband is,' Mary said. Jasper took the chair closest to her on the sofa and the two of them discussed Richard, leaving Silas to Lottie.

'How did you find the daughter of an earl in America?' Lottie's question was straightforward and indelicate in the way only a younger sister's could be. 'The hoi polloi don't usually allow their daughters to wander about like that to be picked up by any old flotsam, no matter who our grandfather is.'

'I'll leave that to Mary to explain if she

decides to engage in any feminine talk with you—after all, you're both married women.' Silas took his sister's hands. 'It's hard to believe you and Millie are married. I wish I could've been here for the weddings.'

'You were with us in spirit, you always are. But don't worry, there are still bills to be paid from all the recent nuptials. You can be with us in that, too.'

'Speaking of which, where is Mother?'

'Silas!' His mother's voice rang out as if she'd heard people speaking about her.

She entered the room, her green eyes boring into him with the same seriousness as when she'd faced him in the hallway outside his father's sick room. The Foundation and everyone in it fell away and Silas was fifteen again, the weight of a world he did not want settling hard on his shoulders along with the conflict between following his own path and the one being dictated to him by others.

While his sister was a mature woman now, his mother had changed very little except for the faint lines around her mouth. Her skin was still smooth and her wavy hair still as dark brown as it had been when he was a boy. She was a little thinner and Silas prayed it wasn't from worry over the missing money and possibly losing everything she and his father had worked to create. As Silas strode to her, he looked down on her, having forgotten how short she was compared to him. Silas braced himself as he waited for her greeting, wondering how effusive or restrained it would be. 'Mother, it's good to see you.'

'And you.' She raised her arms to embrace him, then paused as if afraid he might push her away. He didn't and she pulled him close, the slight scent of vanilla and rosewater taking him back to when he was a very small child and a nightmare had woken him and he'd gone to her for comfort. He should have been here to offer her comfort in return. He hadn't been, but he was home now, even if he wasn't entirely sure what that meant for either of them. 'I was so worried when we heard no word from you.'

'Then why didn't you write?' Silas cursed his tongue. They were not minutes together and already the tension was rising. This time it was his fault.

She let go of him and stepped back, the reserve that she employed with Foundation women who had broken the rules coming over her. 'Your sisters wrote. I was doing all I could to make sure we survived on our limited funds.'

This checked Silas's irritation. 'I'll make sure that never happens again and we'll find out what happened to the missing bank drafts and apparently Millie's and Lottie's letters and mine. I never heard anything from anyone until my solicitor called on you and even he was remiss in getting the information to me in a timely fashion.'

'We'll discuss it later, Silas. There's so much else to hear about, isn't there?' She let go of him, a faraway look of disappointment in her eyes. It was the same one that had marred her expression when she'd agreed to find him a place with Jasper's father's engineering company in Liverpool instead of insisting that he remain here. He caught it before she turned to approach Mary and it cut him to the core. She hadn't forgiven him any more than he had forgiven himself. 'Welcome to the family, Lady Mary.'

Mary's stared over Mrs Fairclough's shoulder at Silas in stunned silence as his mother embraced her.

She called me Lady Mary.

Either Mrs Fairclough had been standing at the door listening to their conversation before she'd entered or she already knew Mary by reputation alone. Given her work, it wasn't impossible to think that she kept abreast of who might need her services no matter what class they were part of. It might have been years since Mary's fall, but as she'd told Silas, stories as sensational as hers never died. It was told to young girls as a warning of what could happen to them and everyone knew why certain daughters of titled men who'd once been coveted marriage partners suddenly disappeared and were treated as if they'd never existed.

'It's a pleasure to finally meet you, Mrs Fairclough,' Mary replied as eagerly a she could, trying to curry favour with her new mother-in-law and ignore how brief the embrace was and how guarded Mrs Fairclough remained as she stood across from her, taking her measure.

I was right to be afraid. She doesn't want me in her family.

'It's probably the real reason why we haven't heard from him in so long,' Lottie teased. 'He was too busy with his railroad and his bride.'

The maid entered with tea and Jasper took his leave of them and his wife, having business to attend to in the city, but he promised to return for dinner. While they ate, Lottie told them all about her and Jasper's adventure finding her friend Harriet and everything they'd uncovered during their escapade. Nothing about Lottie's behaviour as she described roping Jasper into visiting some of the seedier parts of London appeared to surprise Silas or Mrs Fairclough. It stunned Mary, though, as it did Mrs Fairclough listening to her daughter's story without sneering in disgust at how she'd risked her reputation to help a fallen woman.

Mrs Fairclough caught Mary's eyes with the same studying expression as before. Mary twisted her teacup in her saucer, wishing she'd stayed in America. She remembered all the times she'd sat with Ruth in church, waiting for people to judge her, afraid they would speak out against her. She'd detested that feeling and by coming back to England she was dealing with it in droves all over again, of having the people who were now her family look askance at her.

She shifted towards Silas on the sofa, wanting to draw comfort and strength from him, but the stiffness of his bearing stopped her from sitting too close. Whatever reservations and regrets Mary had about being here, Silas held some, too, as if he also worried that at any moment this light-hearted gathering could turn to one of accusations and derision. Mary caught his eye and offered him an encouraging smile. He matched it with an answering one of his own, each of them breathing easier because they were not alone.

Lottie, unaware of their awkwardness, finished her story and was about to start another when someone clearing his throat brought their attention to the sitting-room door. A middle-aged man of average height, with blond hair that was more brown than light and who wore a finely tailored if not lesser quality wool suit very much in the current style, stood patiently. Whoever he was, the fact that he had thought so carefully about his attire was clear, even to Mary.

'Mr Edwards, you must meet my brother, Silas.' Lottie jumped up and took the man by the arm and dragged him into the room. He glanced at her fingers as they pressed into his coat sleeve and Mary wondered if he would shake off her grip and accuse her of wrinkling the fabric the way her brother used to do if either Jane or Mary dared to touch him. He didn't, but stiffly followed her to the table to take Jasper's vacated seat. He barely acknowledged Mary or the other women, but fixed on Silas as if he were some interloping suitor, his eyes a strange mixture of one blue and one brown, with one being a touch darker than the other. 'Silas, this is Jerome Edwards, the Foundation's new manager.'

'Mr Fairclough, it's a pleasure to finally meet the man to whom so much of the Foundation's financial success is due,' Mr Edwards offered with all the deference and caution of a butler welcoming a new lord to the manor. 'Septimus always spoke very highly of you.'

Silas shook the man's hand. The new manager was friendly enough, but there was a reservation behind his smile, much like Silas's mother's. Heaven only knew what complaints about Silas's failings his mother must have made to Mr Edwards while they'd endured the last few lean months. 'I'll have to pay Septimus a visit while I'm home. How is he these days?'

'He resides in the country with his sister, away from the foul London air.' Mr Edwards laid one hand on his chest and cast a wistful look at the ceiling. 'It's a life that we can all aspire to.'

'It is. In the meantime, I have some Foundation business to discuss with you,' Silas said, addressing him as he would Mr Hachman. 'Tomorrow, I'd like to meet with you to discuss possible reasons why the bank drafts went missing. I'd also like to review the Foundation accounts to ensure that the Foundation is on solid financial footing. I won't allow this sort of thing to happen again or leave Mother to rely on the Marquess or Jasper for handouts.'

Silas's announcement cleared all pastoral dreams from Mr Edwards's eyes. 'I assure you that the accounts are in perfect order. The trouble must be with the bank.'

'I'll investigate that, too, but I still want to see the accounts so I can best help my mother with the trust I'm establishing for her.' It was a bald-faced lie. While Silas did want to know how best to help his mother, he also wished to make sure that the accounts were in as pristine a shape as Mr Edwards claimed and that nothing more nefarious than a simple mistake with the bank had taken place. He didn't wish to accuse the manager of anything, but he didn't know him well enough to place him above suspicion. 'I'll also be appointing a trustee, someone like Jasper who can act as my agent and can keep on top of things so that if there is trouble I'm not learning about it six months later from some solicitor with no personal interest in the matter.'

Mr Edwards exchanged an almost-indignant look with Silas's mother, visibly struggling against his shock to maintain his deference. 'Of course. Your mother and the Foundation's well-being are of the utmost concern to all of us. If you'll excuse me, I have accounts to attend to.'

Mr Edwards bowed and took his leave.

'You were very curt with Mr Edwards,' Silas's mother remarked, as pleased as Mr Edwards had been about Silas's announcements.

'It's nothing more than business. As a manager, he should understand that.'

'Of course, but we can't have him thinking that he's being accused of anything either,' his mother warned in a soft but firm voice that made it clear that Silas was not to jeopardise Mr Edwards's employment. 'The Foundation is a welcoming place for everyone in need of help, including Mr Edwards. He fell on hard time when he lost his last position because his prior employer made too many bad investments.'

'Then he of all people should welcome the security of steady funds from a trust,' Silas shot back, irked that his mother seemed more concerned with keeping Mr Edwards than the roof over her head.

'He will, if you phrase it with a little more delicacy.'

Silas didn't answer and the awkward strain that had marred the first moments of their reunion returned, so much so that Lottie shot Mary a discomforting look before she broke in with her bright voice.

'I'm sure Mr Edwards will do everything he can to help Silas avoid such problems in the future. He wants as much as we do for the Foundation to succeed. In the meantime, tell us about your railroad, Silas.'

* * *

Mary listened while Silas told them about the Baltimore Southern Railway, the stiffness in his back from his mother's rebuke easing as he described his work with the same energy that had convinced his investors to part with money for the foundry.

'I knew you'd put all that charm to good use one day,' Lottie teased, as captivated as Mary by her successful brother. Preston had never done anything more than stand to inherit an estate, biding his time until he'd became a viscount by gambling and running up debts that Jane had written to her about much later. Mary could see from this simple house and neighbourhood how far Silas had raised himself through his efforts and it increased her admiration for him.

Mrs Fairclough was much more reserved in her reaction and it tempered some of Silas's natural enthusiasm. Mary wondered if it was a true lack of interest in his success or that he'd marred it through his poor choice of bride that made his mother withhold effusive praise. Whatever it was, Mary hoped that the undercurrent of tension between them could be resolved by the time they returned to America. She knew what it was to have the weight of her parent's disappointment dragging at her. She didn't wish to add Mrs Fairclough's to it or for Silas to come to resent Mary for being the cause of it.

Chapter Nine

Silas led Mary into his old bedroom, ready for the night. Jasper had joined them for dinner as promised, but they had yet to see Millie and her illustrious husband. Silas was glad the Marquess hadn't been there. After their long travels and the reunion that had been both joyous and discomforting, Silas was in no mood to charm a man. It was a rare occasion when he sought solitude instead of company, especially as he set his lamp down on the top of the old dresser. It had once held his model soldier collection until he'd replaced it with small replicas of steam engines. The toys had been sold ages ago for their lead to help pay for necessities after his father had died.

Silas breathed in the slight mustiness from the damp old wood, the faint smoke from a chimney that sometimes didn't clear, and felt the lumpiness of the knotted rug under his feet. Little about the room had changed in the past ten years and the part of him that enjoyed a well-appointed room in Baltimore rebelled at the puritan simplicity, especially as Mary searched through her leather and wood trunk. She deserved more, Silas had worked for more and yet this was home.

'Are you all right, Silas?' Mary faced him, her fine night things draped over one arm.

'I always imagined I'd return, but it's hard to believe I'm here. There are so many memories. Not all of them are good.' Comfort hung in the air along with the recollection of reading about the latest in steam innovation, dreaming of the railroads and attending to his studies with his father standing over him. It was kneeling beside the turned wood bed praying that his father would live so that he could make peace with him that made it hard to be here. His father hadn't survived, stealing Silas's chance at forgiveness and changing everything.

Mary didn't ask for more and he stared into her round brown eyes. She understood better than he could place into words the conflict between being home and wanting to be anywhere else. Here, the old failures settled around him like the dust not even a good cleaning could clear from the room after all these years. He longed to tell Mary of the argument with his father about Silas wanting to work for the railway instead of the Foundation, of his father accusing him of being as grasping as the grandfather Silas had never met and the ugly words of frustration that Silas had hurled at him in return. Then he'd stalked off to find employment anyway. It was Millie who'd found him at the railway yard a week later to tell him their father had caught typhoid and it was dire. It didn't matter that Silas had returned home immediately. His father had never come out of his delirium long enough for Silas to know if he ever forgave him. He was too ashamed to reveal it, especially since he'd made the same mistake again, quarrelling with his mother about his future, thinking he had no way forward but to run off to America, leaving her with nothing more than a letter he knew she'd receive long after he was at sea, swearing Jasper to secrecy so no one could stop him. These acts of cowardice clung to him so tightly that even his successes couldn't peel them off as his unease during tea and dinner and in his mother's presence had reminded him. 'My mother wasn't exactly enamoured of my success tonight.'

It was as close to the truth as he was willing to venture. Mary would think less of him if he told her the details about his leaving for America. After having her fiancé walk away from her, he refused to give her any reason to believe that he might do the same to her some day. Silas was an honourable man who upheld his promises to himself and others. He shouldn't allow one act of cowardice to define him, but it was easier to say than it was to believe it.

'Your sister is over the moon that we're here.'

'It'll be hard on her when we leave again.' He would make a better effort with his departure this time, but he still worried that his family would view it as him turning his back on them. There'd been no mistaking his mother's reference to his prior departure during tea. It'd confirmed every suspicion he'd had that she hadn't forgiven him for leaving. She might not again, but he must go. His life was in America.

'It'll give my mother another reason to be disappointed in me.'

'I think it's me she's disappointed in. She wasn't any more ecstatic about my presence than she was your railroad.' Mary sat down on the edge of the bed, dropping her nightgown beside her, her dejection troubling him.

He sat down beside her. 'Don't worry about that, it's just her way. She takes the measure of everyone who comes here.'

'Then maybe that's her way with you, too, especially since you've been gone for so long. You've changed and she doesn't know how to approach it or you.'

'Not my mother. She's spent her life solving problems for others and the Foundation.' He tugged loose the cravat knot and unwound the silk from around his neck. 'If anyone can adjust to change, it's her. She's had no choice but to do so.'

'It doesn't mean she likes it or doesn't struggle with it like we do.'

'No, I don't suppose it does.' Silas undid his coat and slipped it off. Mary was right. His mother had endured a great deal of change after his father had passed and she'd been forced to face more of it in the last few weeks. Perhaps she was struggling as much as he and, as hard as it was to imagine, maybe she didn't know what to do any more than he did. However, it still didn't explain why she hadn't written to him over the years or in the last few months when they were all in doubt about his health and whereabouts. He turned to Mary and brushed a curl away from her face, leaving his hand to linger on her cheek, her skin warm and soft beneath his. 'I'm glad Richard sent you here.'

'So am I.' He kissed her, running his fingers through Mary's hair and dislodging a number of pins that plinked against the floorboards at their feet. He slid his arm around her waist and drew her close, craving the arch of her body against his. She was everything he was now instead of the past, a way to taste and touch the new world they had left behind in Baltimore. Her embrace and her words gave him back the pride that made him walk with his head held high in Maryland and to look people like Mr Penniman straight in the eye and convince them that their money was well spent with him. In the light brush of her fingertips against the skin on the back of his neck lay all the dreams he had accomplished in a few short years and all the ones he still had left to pursue. He would not fail, but continue to be the successful man she'd married, even here where the past tried to pull him down.

Mary lay in Silas's arms, listening to the early morning sounds of London outside the window. She'd slept a good portion of the night, the train ride here and the apprehension of meeting his family and their lovemaking having left her exhausted. Then the familiar clop of horses and the rattle of carts on the street before sunrise as the bakers and the brewers had begun their day had awakened her. This part of London was so different than the one she'd grown up in, but the sounds were familiar in a way they had not been in Baltimore or even in the country with Ruth.

She'd found peace in Silas's arms last night, but now she was wary. In America, she'd been given the chance to reinvent herself. Then, before she'd really embraced the opportunity, she'd been pulled back to England. Despite his assurances that his mother was reserved with everyone that came to the Foundation, she still couldn't help but think that she wasn't pleased with her new daughter-in-law. She wanted her mother-in-law to like her or at least be happy that Silas was married and not recoil from her the way her own family had done. Silas might dismiss her aloofness, but if it continued, the unease that had troubled Silas when they'd first come up to this room after dinner would plague him again, only this time she would be to blame for it.

He'd blame her even more if her past spread out to harm his sisters or the Foundation. His sister was the Marchioness of Falconmore. Mary couldn't remember if her parents had any connection to the Falconmores, but if they did they wouldn't appreciate having this old skeleton from the family closet reappearing at a ball any more than Lord Falconmore was likely to enjoy discovering that he was now related by marriage to a notorious woman. Lord Falconmore must have heard about her and what had happened. It would make things difficult for Silas's sister, too. A woman of her simple background must already be struggling against the prejudices of the aristocracy to settle into her new role. It would become a great deal harder for her if everyone looked askance at her because of her fallen sister-in-law.

No, I won't let that happen.

She had to make sure that Silas and his family didn't pay the price for her past mistakes or have their reputation and that of the Foundation's tarnished because of her. They, like all charitable foundations, relied on wealthy donors to keep them going. If they tied themselves to a woman like her, those donors might take their funds elsewhere. Silas was here to help his family in a time of need, she didn't wish to create more need for them or to ruin their chances for patrons the way she'd ruined her brother's marriage prospects. Silas might be able to ignore her past when it was just the two of them, but if it hurt his sisters or mother it might cost her the affection and concern of a man she'd grown to care a great deal about in so short an amount of time.

She watched Silas sleep peacefully beside her, his strong profile highlighted by the glowing coals in the fireplace. She might have approached this marriage with no intention of losing her heart to him, but the more time that went by, the more she realised that not falling for him was impossible. He was too good a man to remain distant from, too caring and concerned about her for her to wall off her heart from him. Not since Ruth had anyone tried to build her up or encourage her to think more of herself than society wanted her to the way he did. He helped her believe in their future together and it was one she wanted to share with him more than she had wanted almost anything else in a long time. She couldn't lose it and him. She would have to devise some reason why she couldn't go to Millie's wedding ball, one that didn't make her look like a coward and one that Silas couldn't dismiss with his usual optimism. She'd also have to think of some way to avoid meeting Lord Falconmore. It would involve lying to Silas and his family by making up mysterious illnesses that kept her in bed while they dined downstairs, but it must be done. For the first time since she'd seen Silas on the dock in Liverpool, she questioned Richard's wisdom in sending her here. Richard had been gone from England for too long and had forgotten how it really was here, that the principles that made America a land of opportunity did not exist in aristocratic London. She hadn't forgotten. She never could.

Chapter Ten

'Good morning, Mr Edwards,' Silas greeted when he entered his small office at the back of the Foundation that sat adjacent to the Fairclough home. A door connected the two buildings, helping to maintain some distance between Silas's family's work and their personal lives. Silas had risen early, determined to address the issue of the ledger and missing money before his mother could object.

Mr Edwards set down his pen, closed the ledger and rose to greet Silas. 'Good morning, Mr Fairclough. You're up early.' Despite his smile, he eyed Silas as if he were a dog unsure whether or not to accept a treat from a stranger.

'I'm always up early, as my mother assured me you are, too.' She'd been very careful at dinner to tell Silas how conscientious a man

Mr Edwards was when it came to Foundation affairs, still more worried about losing Mr Edwards than losing Silas's money.

'I find myself most productive in the quiet hours of the morning before the many interruptions that tend to come throughout the day.' Mr Edwards tugged at his shirt cuffs and Silas noted the fine gold cufflinks holding them closed. They matched the gold chain and pocket watch dangling from his well-cut waistcoat. Not only did the man like to rise early, but he liked to be well turned out. Mr Edwards noticed Silas studying his cufflinks. 'They were my father's. He was a man of money, but he lost it in a bad business venture. The cottage we had in the country was sold and we were forced to come to London. Sadly, my father found gin before he found work, leaving it to me to support my mother. These and a few other trinkets are all that's left, the only things my mother hid so my father couldn't sell them. As you know, it's difficult to live in London without money, to hover just above the penury that's merely a street from here, knowing that you're only one misfortune away from sinking in to it.'

'Of that I am all too familiar.'

'Thankfully, my mother is no longer here to see me brought so low once again. If it wasn't for Mrs Fairclough hiring me, I would have faced ruin after my last employer fled to France to avoid paying his outstanding bills, including my wages.'

'She is very generous to those in need.' Not so much to Silas who'd made as many mistakes as most of the people here and was just as in need of her forgiveness and understanding.

'I hope to get away from all of this misery some day, to return to the country where it's peaceful and beautiful. I miss it.'

Silas recognised the manager's dream. It was the yearning for a different life that had driven Silas to America, and the reason he was here this morning, to ensure his mother never slipped into the poverty surrounding them, the one she'd helped so many avoid. 'I'd like to see the ledgers you've kept for the last six months and for you to help me understand the expenses and revenue.'

'You can't possibly believe that I'm involved in the missing money?' Mr Edwards asked as horrified as he'd been last night when Silas had mentioned the trust.

'Of course not, I simply want to understand how things are run,' Silas lied through a pang of guilt. His mother was no fool and he doubted that a man Septimus had recommended, and who worked closely with his mother every day, could be deceiving them. This should be enough to ease Silas's worries, but it wasn't and wouldn't be until he got to the bottom of the matter. He wanted to make sure that there were no discrepancies in the ledgers, nothing to indicate that the money hadn't merely gone missing, but had been pilfered.

'Of course,' Mr Edwards agreed but before he could open the ledger, the swish of a woman's skirt and the firm notes of Silas's mother's voice sounded in the room.

'Silas, might I have a word with you?' Silas's mother stood in the office doorway, having surprised him like she used to do whenever Silas and his sisters would hide under the stairs to plot a raid on the kitchen.

Silas tried not to grind his teeth as he followed his mother down the hallway to a small sitting room that was sparse and dark, the fire not having been lit yet to save money on coal. 'Is something wrong?'

'You know how it is for the people who come here, the difficulties and prejudices they've endured and the second chance we offer free of judgement.'

'I do.'

'Mr Edwards is one of those people and I won't have you casting aspersions on him by questioning him about the accounts. I ask you to begin your investigation elsewhere— the bank, perhaps.'

'I will, as soon as possible, but as it's a bank holiday, I can't do it today. In the meantime, I wish to start here.'

'This is your home, Silas, and you are always welcome here, but the Foundation isn't your railroad.' She didn't snap at him, that wasn't her way, but she was as firm and direct with him as he was with the men he sometimes had to let go.

'It is my money and I want to know where it went.'

His mother took a deep breath, settling herself the way she used to do whenever he or his sisters failed to see reason in any argument.

Silas and Lottie had received far more of those looks than Millie ever had. 'I understand your concern, but you must remember your place. You cannot appear unannounced and interfere with the running of the Foundation.'

'There was a time when the only thing you wanted from me was my involvement in the Foundation,' he snapped. This wasn't how he wished to approach the situation. He would prefer to handle it with a cool head and even temper as he would any problem with the Baltimore Southern. In front of his mother it seemed he could do neither.

'It was, but you made your decision and we both must live with it, even now.'

Silas pressed his fists to his hips, feeling more like the fifteen-year-old boy who'd tried and failed to make his mother see reason when it came to his desire to work with the railroads, leaving him no choice but to sneak away. She refused to see why he needed to get involved in the Foundation's affairs after years of avoiding it, but he was hesitant to press too hard, afraid the argument that had been delayed by the Atlantic Ocean and a number of years would rear its ugly head. It wasn't a discussion he wished to have at any time, much less the morning after his arrival. 'Then may I have your permission to review the ledgers?'

His mother touched the back of her hair, adjusting the pin holding the chignon tight. He remembered that gesture well from his childhood, it was the one she'd done whenever something someone said or did troubled her deeply, the one that occurred before the end of any disagreeable conversation. 'You've had a long journey and been greeted with so many changes since you stepped through the door. We can discuss this further in a few days when you are better rested and we are at less of a risk of saying things we may regret.'

He didn't press the matter because she was right. He'd come home out of concern and love for his family. He didn't wish to misspeak and drive a wedge between them more than his having gone to America had already done. This time he wanted to leave with happy memories instead of conflict and regret. 'All right, we'll deal with this at another time. If you'll excuse me.'

Silas stepped past his mother, but her voice made him stop at the door.

'I am happy to see you, Silas. We've missed you very much.'

The words were heartfelt and they cut Silas deeper than any of her criticism or resistance to his investigation could have. He'd been a coward to leave without telling her or his sisters—to walk away from them the way Mary's faithless lover had walked away from her—leaving them in doubt of the true depths of his concern, but he'd felt so trapped here in England, suffocated by the inability to act and do and strive for everything he'd wanted, and by the regret of never having made peace with his father.

'I'm glad to be here.' And he was, even while he longed for America.

Mary finished the last of her breakfast, having come downstairs shortly after Silas had risen. Despite his efforts to dress quietly and not disturb her, his agitated movements and the soft but steady pacing around the room as he'd gathered his things had woken her. She'd come downstairs, ready to assist him. Judging by the tight line of his lips, he did need her.

'Is everything well?' She wondered if he'd

discovered some discrepancy in the accounts already.

'My mother and I did not see eye to eye on my need to review the ledgers.'

'Perhaps after some time to think about it she'll change her mind.'

'We'll see. My mother can be a very stubborn woman.' He opened his arms to the room. 'One has to be to run a place like this.'

Mary came around the table and adjusted his cravat. 'I think you inherited it from her, along with her persistence.'

'In Baltimore I would have said that was a good thing, but not here.'

'Surely Mr Edwards isn't in the office all the time, nor is your mother,' she suggested, looking up at him through her lashes.

Silas huffed. 'My mother has that instinct that all mothers have for knowing when their children are up to something,'

'My mother never had that instinct.' If she had, maybe she would have noticed all the nights Mary had slipped out of Foxcomb Hall or the mornings when she'd been more tired than after a ball. It was difficult for a mother to be attentive when her rooms were half a mile away in a whole different wing of the house. If it hadn't been for her lady's maid and the other servants, Mary could have expired in her rooms and no one would have found her body for days.

'Mine excels in it.'

'Even when she's asleep?' Mary asked with a touch of mischief that made Silas tilt his head at her. If there was one thing her misguided time with Preston had taught her it was how to sneak about and not get caught. Her pride in this sad accomplishment threatened to vanish. If she had been caught, then everything would have been different. Although with Silas looking at her like the devil for being so clever she was glad things had worked out as they had.

He slipped his arms around her waist and pulled her against him. 'Are you suggesting we stay up late tonight for other reasons besides the marriage bed?'

Mary didn't blush at Silas's bold statement. There was no reason to be coy with her husband. The lady's magazines might suggest that husbands preferred wives who pretended at innocence, but Mary wasn't about to play such games, especially with a man who had no need for them. 'Perhaps we may engage in marriage-bed activities before a touch of light reading in Mr Edwards's office, assuming he doesn't sleep too close to his books.'

'His bedroom is on the other side of the Foundation building, away from any temptation that might distract him from his figures.'

'Figures are exactly what we're interested in,' she purred in his ear, her breath making the short hair at his temple ruffle. It would be far too many hours until they were alone together tonight.

'Indeed, we are.' He nuzzled her neck, raising a chill along her spine.

She tilted her head back to enjoy the heat of his lips as he trailed soft kisses along her cheeks before claiming her mouth. To indulge in something this wicked which was no longer wicked was heaven. It was the one thing about the many sins she'd made all those years ago—she'd enjoyed it, until she hadn't. She pushed the thought aside, opening her mouth to accept Silas's tongue, her fingers tightening on Silas's firm arm through his fine coat. There was no sin in enjoying this.

The clank of a coal bucket in the sitting room as the maid attended to the fireplace made them jump apart.

'Until tonight,' Silas said with some regret, but more of the enthusiasm that Mary had come to cherish. 'It's our first full day in London, what shall we do?'

'I thought you were going to visit Mr Williams about the engine.'

'Not until this afternoon. This morning, I want to get out and see the sights.'

'Then let's go.'

The hack rolled to a stop in a section of London Mary didn't recognise. There was so much of the city she'd failed to see when she'd lived here, her entire world circumscribed by the rules of the Season and the invisible boundaries of polite society. All around them surged a tide of people and the usual noises of a London street, the clop of horses' hooves and the creaking of carriage wheels, the calling of hawkers and people to one another as they went about their business. Beneath the cacophony was the steady thump of something large and mechanical from somewhere up ahead. Beneath it was the familiar whoosh and hiss of what sounded like one of the steam engines of Silas and Richard's Baltimore Southern Railway.

'You'll see.' Silas led her through the crowd towards the noise, his gloved hand holding on tight to hers, unwilling to lose her in the crush. They stopped at a wrought-iron railing protecting them from the large hole in the ground. There were numerous other people pressed up against it and looking down into the earth, including ragamuffin street children standing beside finely dressed gentleman. Mary looked fast at the men in their smartly tailored suits and top hats, terrified they might be someone she'd once known. She couldn't imagine an aristocrat sullying his boots with mud from this part of town, but the wonder in the ground before them might be tempting enough for one or two of them to venture a little further than Hyde Park. The chances it would be this early in the morning weren't likely. Those in town at this time of year must still be in bed sleeping off their night at White's or some other less reputable club. Still, the panic that had seized her left her tired when it dissipated. This wasn't how she wanted to live, constantly afraid that every well-dressed man who walked by might be someone she'd known or that each woman who turned to reveal the face inside the fashionable bonnet might sneer at her. It made her wish she didn't have to leave Silas's family's house, but even there she wasn't safe. Eventually, Silas's sister Millie would show up with her husband and then the real trouble would begin.

'Is everything all right?' Silas wrapped his arm around her waist. His ability to notice her moods before she could say anything had been endearing in Baltimore, but at this moment was most inconvenient.

'Everything is fine, only this sight is so overwhelming,' she lied, turning to peer into the large hole in the earth, eager to shift his attention from her to where they were. 'What is it?'

'The first tunnel underneath the Thames. Mr Brunel designed and built it, after one he built in Russia. Steam engines make it possible to dig, along with numerous other building techniques he's developed. With this technology, imagine what we'll be able to do with railroads in America. Rivers and large mountains will no longer be an obstacle in the way of progress, but simply another portion of the railway to be built.'

Mary looked down at the circular opening. Classical swags had been carved into the cement work supporting the sides of the hole, and long, curving staircases wound down into the ground before opening up into the tunnel that led beneath the river. The mildew scent of water and mud drifted up along with the chatter of workmen and the clank of bricks and chisels.

'When I was younger, I used to come here sometimes. They charged a shilling to go down and watch the workers. I never had the money to pay to see the steam engine up close, but I once convinced a worker to let me in, to marvel at everything they were doing, to dream that I could accomplish such impossible things the way Mr Brunel did.'

'And you have.' Mary squeezed Silas's arm in encouragement.

'And I'll do even more when I have the English steam-engine patent.'

'You'll get it, I'm sure you will.'

Silas turned his back on the tunnel and

rested his thighs against the railing as he faced her. 'I've shown you want I wanted to see, what would you like to do now? We can go anywhere.'

Except places where anyone I used to know might be, Mary wanted to say, but bit her tongue, refusing to dampen the delight of the morning.

She was eager to enjoy her time with him, to see more of the sparkling Silas instead of the sober one who had greeted her in the dining room this morning or before they'd made love last night. He was as troubled as her by this homecoming, as conflicted as she was about a past that could never truly be resolved. They both needed to forget it all for a while.

'Show me some more of the city that I might never have seen before, things you used to love and enjoy.'

'Even if it's noisy and dirty and full of people?'

'Especially if it's noisy and dirty and full of people.'

He escorted her away from the Thames Tunnel. They approached a man dressed in rags who held out his hand to beg for a coin from the many men and women who passed him without a glance. Silas dug into his pocket for a shilling and laid it in the man's grimy palm, not recoiling at this smudge of dirt the man's fingers left on his fine leather glove.

'Thank you, sir, and God bless,' the man said.

Silas tipped his hat to him, showing him the same respect he would any other gentleman before he and Mary continued. 'Well, what do you want to do?'

'Let's go to Mr J. R. Smith's Tour of Europe Panorama. I used to beg my parents to take me to see it whenever we were in London, but they wouldn't. They were too afraid of breathing common air to dream of mixing with the rabble.'

'Then the Panorama it is.'

Chapter Eleven

Mary let out a deep sigh as she sat in the front window of the Fairclough house watching the traffic on the street outside pass by, wishing Silas were here. After a delightful morning together, he'd left her to meet with Mr Williams about the English steam-engine patent. Mary had spent a good hour unpacking her and Silas's things, refusing to add additional work to the young maid's already full day. With everything arranged in the wardrobe and the dresser, there was nothing else for Mary to do but come downstairs. The house was quiet with Lottie being at her own home and Mrs Fairclough engaged in whatever Foundation business occupied her day.

More than once Mary considered going through the small hall to the adjoining Foundation house and offering her help, but each time she hesitated, afraid of Mrs Fairclough's judgement. From what Mary had already seen of the woman, and everything she'd built and maintained through hardship and lean times, Mrs Fairclough was as strong and determined as her son. She wasn't formidable in the way Preston's mother had been, but it was clear there was steeliness beneath her gentleness that one would be foolish to overlook.

Mary should have taken the risk of Mrs Fairclough's judgement instead of lingering here with the newspaper. She'd make the mistake of reading it and most of the people mentioned in the society column she only knew in passing from when she'd lived in England. It was the last paragraph at the bottom that had nearly stopped her heart and made her long for Silas's sure presence. In bold, typewritten letters Mary had read about the birth of Jane's first child, the next Earl of Longford, that the christening would be held soon and that both the Ashfords and the Longfords were proud grandparents.

Mary would not be there for the christening or for any other event in her nephew's life.

In none of Jane's recent letters had she mentioned being with child, but with Mary having gone to America, Jane's letters had taken so much longer to reach her. No doubt the missive with the news would be waiting for her when she returned to Baltimore. Mary considered writing a letter of congratulations to her sister, of telling her she was in London and asking if she could come visit her and the new baby, but she didn't. Even if Jane was willing to accept Mary into her home, the Earl of Longford wasn't likely to countenance Mary darkening his doorstep. Jane was celebrating the triumphant birth of a son and heir, a wanted child who would secure her place in the Longford family, unlike Mary, whose child would only have been accepted if she'd faced Preston across the anvil. Even then the truth of its conception would have followed it and her for the rest of their lives, especially if the child had been a girl. It didn't matter. The child hadn't lived and she and Preston had not married.

Tears filled Mary's eyes as every loss she'd endured over the last four years threatened to overwhelm her in the fog and smoke laden air of London.

'Good afternoon, Lady Mary,' Mrs Fairclough greeted, stealing as silently into the room as she had last night, her plain dress barely rustling with her steady and stately stride. If Silas hadn't told Mary during the train ride about his mother's simple background as the daughter of a tradesman inventor, Mary would've thought her far more high born. Mary wondered if she'd ever struggled in the same way she did with her change in status and the direction in which her life had gone. 'I hope you don't feel that I'm neglecting you?'

It was a far warmer greeting than Mary had received yesterday and it set some of her fears at ease. Mrs Fairclough wasn't going to berate her for her past sins while Silas was gone, at least not yet.

'Of course not, I know you have a great deal to do and it's been rather nice to sit here in the quiet after so much travelling.' Mary tried as sneakily as she could to brush away the moisture clouding her visions. She didn't want Mrs Fairclough to ask why she was moping in the sitting room. Mary was too afraid she wouldn't be able to keep all the truths inside her from pouring out if she did, giving the woman every reason to shun Mary. However, she knew as well as Mrs Fairclough did that she was failing to hide the tears.

'Perhaps you'd like to help me with some of our work. Today we're giving sewing lessons to the women. It's what we do, prepare the women for some kind of future other than the one their status has enforced on them. Can you sew?'

'I do a fine stitch.' There hadn't been much else to do in the country but sew.

'Then come with me.'

Mary followed her, thankful Mrs Fairclough hadn't asked anything more personal about Mary than her abilities with the needle. They walked down the hall of the house to the door connecting it to the brick building that sat adjacent to it. Where the Faircloughs' house was cosy like a family's, the Foundation's had more of the air of an institution about it. The furniture was built for utility rather than decoration and the art on the walls and the knick-knacks on the various side tables were few and far between, keeping everything uncluttered. That was not to say it was cold or foreboding like a work house for it wasn't. It was a welcoming space, but one that was a place for people to stay temporarily until they could move on to a better situation.

'It's quiet at this time of day. The women who've been here longer have gone out to their positions as seamstresses or in service and some of them will be moving on from here shortly. The older women who reside with us serve as our matrons. They are servants who worked a long time with a family and were dismissed, through no fault of their own, with no reference or position, such as Mr Edwards,' Mrs Fairclough explained, the pride in her voice at the Foundation's accomplishments evident. 'Today, we're honing our sewing in the dining room where we often work when we need to spread out.'

Mrs Fairclough led Mary into the dining room. It was a much simpler room than the Faircloughs' one with the large table in the centre covered in a clutter of fabric, needles, pins, thread and ribbons. Four young women and two older ones looked up from their work when Mary walked in. She halted over the threshold, almost afraid to join them. They all seemed so young, the same age as Mary had been when her misfortunes had befallen her. Mary's heart began to race as she thought of the morning her parents had ordered her lady's maid to pack up her things, giving her only the basics to take with her, forcing her to leave behind the beautiful gowns and fine gloves. They'd told her she wouldn't need them where she was going and she'd stood shaking in fear, terrified they would order her dropped off in some unknown part of the city where she would be left to fend for herself. Thankfully, they'd sent her to Ruth, who had calmed her fears with hugs and helped to dry her tears.

'Ladies, this is Lady Mary Fairclough, my son Silas's wife. She's going to help us with our work today.'

The women rose to their feet and said in unison, 'Good morning, Lady Mary.'

Mary wanted to yell at them to sit down and not show her respect, she didn't deserve it because she was no different than they, but then Silas's words came back to her.

Don't think about who you were but who you are, the wife of a prosperous Baltimore businessman.

Yes, she was, and like these women who

were working to put their mistakes behind them, so was she. Perhaps it would help them to see all that they might achieve in spite of their misfortunes, but Mary didn't have the courage to admit that she was no different than they. She didn't want their respect for her to change into disdain. Instead, she nodded kindly the way she imagined any other generous patroness who entered here might do.

Mrs Fairclough urged Mary to sit down and within a few minutes, after introductions and some explanation of their work, Mary set to stitching a fine hem on a small girl's dress.

Mary sewed in silence, listening to the young women talk among themselves of neighbourhood gossip and family news. Mrs Fairclough oversaw their progress, going to each woman and enquiring about their day or how they were and helping to correct their stitches. Mary wondered how her future might have been if she hadn't had Ruth or a place like this in which to seek shelter. Mary touched the watch hanging on the new chain from the bodice of her dress. Ruth had never judged her, but simply accepted her and her mistakes while urging her to remain strong and endure whatever happened to her and to have faith that all would be well in the end. Mary was still waiting to see if that would ultimately be true.

Mrs Fairclough came around the table to Mary, admiring her work as she had the other women's with an approving nod. 'You are good with a needle. Did your mother teach you?'

'No, Mrs Fairclough.' Mary concentrated on the push and pull of the needle through the fabric so that her face gave no indication of how much she did not wish to think of her mother at this moment or to have Mrs Fairclough ask any more questions about her past. She didn't want to lie to her, but she could not tell her the truth. 'My companion for a number of years used to sew layettes for the poor mothers of the village or clothes for their children. I used to help her and she and I worked very hard to refine my stitch. She also taught me to keep simple accounts.'

She noticed two of the Foundation women exchanging curious glances, no doubt wondering what a woman with the honourarium Lady affixed to her name would be doing with a companion, especially one who'd taught her such practical skills.

'Please, call me Lilian.' Mrs Fairclough sat down in the chair beside her. 'Those skills are very much in demand here, aren't they, Mrs Bethany?'

'Yes, they are,' the plump matron with grey hair answered before leaning over to correct one of the women's stitches.

'Perhaps you wouldn't mind imparting what you know to our guests while you're here. We can use all the help we can get.'

'I'd be delighted.' It was the least Mary could do to show these women kindness and to help them the way Ruth had helped her.

Lilian sat down beside her and took up an embroidery hoop. Thankfully, she didn't ask Mary any questions about her companion or her life when she'd lived in England, but listened like Mary did to the other women chatting, their lively discussions covering the quiet between the two women. Lilian drew a long line of thread through her embroidery fabric before tucking the needle back through. The scene she embroidered was a whimsical one of unicorns and a magical forest, the image a stark contrast between the sensible small stitches and the woman in the dark dress making them. Perhaps Lilian understood Silas better than he realised, but of course Mary was being silly. It was nothing but embroidery.

Mary worked hard on the dress, enjoying the companionship of the others and the distraction from thinking of Jane when Lilian's question dragged her back into the room and reality.

'I understand from Lottie that you're Lord Ashford's daughter.' Lilian lowered her voice, doing her best to keep the conversation between them and out of earshot of the rest of the room.

'I am.' Mary's heart thumped against the inside of her chest, not wanting her mother-in-law to discover that Mary was the same as the women sitting around them. No doubt she'd already guessed and she would upbraid her in front of all these women, bringing her as low as her family once had for her mistakes.

'Will you visit your family while you're here?'

Mary pinched the needle tight, afraid she might drop it. 'No, I haven't spoken to my family for many years.'

'I see.' Lilian glanced past Mary to the other

women before fixing on Mary, her voice low and soothing. Mary's finger shook as she pushed the needle through the fabric, her stitches growing sloppier with each moment she waited for Lilian to unmask her as a fraud pretending to be a lady and to accuse her of dragging her son down into the filth he'd risen up from. Lilian did neither, but tilted closer to Mary. 'The one thing I tell the women we take in after I interview them to find out their stories is that they are not alone. It may feel as though they are, as if the world has ended and no one understands their suffering, but it isn't true. There are many women that have gone before them and many women who will come after them, not just here but all over London and other places. I don't ever want anyone here to feel ashamed or unwanted and judged because of their mistakes, because here they aren't. Do you understand?'

Mary lowered the dress and nodded, not trusting her voice enough to respond.

'Whatever your story, Mary, whether you decide to tell me or not, it doesn't matter. All I wish is for you is to be a good wife to my son, to support him in ways I perhaps failed to do, to make sure he's happy with the decisions he's made and the life he's chosen to lead.'

'I will,' Mary promised, noticing the veil of tears glimmering in Lilian's eyes. Whatever distance and tension there was between mother and son, it was clear they both loved one another a great deal even when they did not see eye to eye. It heartened Mary to believe that these kind of families existed. After the coldness of hers it gave her hope that her own future might involve more care and love than she'd dared to imagine when she'd stood with Silas before the Justice of the Peace.

Silas sat across the desk from Mr Williams, his usual confidence that had almost been shaken out of him by his confrontation with his mother this morning with him once again. 'America is in need of an engine with the power to haul increasing amounts of goods and people. I can assure you handsome profits from the lease of your patent and help you secure your reputation as one of the finest engine designers in the world.'

Mr Cooper, Mr Williams's assistant, sat at his desk off to the side, listening to the conversation and taking copious notes, at least that's what Silas assumed he was writing furiously while Silas and Mr Williams spoke. For all he knew, the clerk was drafting some legal document.

'And when my model becomes obsolete?' Mr Williams straightened the pens in the stand again. He was a slender man with thinning blond hair and spectacles pushed high up on the bridge of his nose. He sat, but he hadn't been still the entire time. Silas wondered if he yelled 'boo' whether Mr Williams would flee, he was that agitated and restless.

'A man like you will never be out of new idea to replace the old ones. You'll give us enough new engines to keep us going for many years and through many different developments.'

Silas's confidence in Mr Williams did nothing to bolster Mr Williams's. He touched the pens again, knocking them out of their previous perfect alignment. 'But with you in America I'll have no oversight over the quality of the production of my designs. I can't have inferior copies ruining my company's good name.'

'My desire for quality matches yours, it's

the reason I wish to produce the engines in America where I can be involved in every step of the process, from using the finest steel for construction to making sure the best metal workers are employed. I can't afford inferior engines that'll burst boilers the first time they traverse a steep incline in cold weather. I need a sturdy, reliable engine, a true workhorse. I need yours.'

Mr Williams glanced at his assistant, who momentarily looked up from his work at the mention of Mr Williams's designs before ducking back down to concentrate on his paper. Silas didn't care what silent exchange took place between them. What interested him was that Mr Williams made no move for the pens, giving him some hope that he'd finally won the man over, until he spoke. 'That's all well and good, but what's to stop you from taking my designs and passing them off as your own?'

Silas almost sighed in frustration. Not even investors were ever this difficult to woo. 'I don't dabble in such underhanded dealings.'

'So you say, but I have nothing but your word to assure me.' Mr Williams straightened the pens again, making them stand perfectly upright. 'I can't tell you how many men have come in here and given me their word only to betray me. I, and especially my investors, will need something more concrete than your promises.'

'Do you know who Jasper King is, who his father was?' Silas was reluctant to name his now very close family connection, wanting to stand on his own merit as he'd wanted to do in Baltimore, but if it won him the patent, then so be it. He had to overcome Mr Williams's objections.

The man's eyes went wide at the mention of King Enterprises and he and Mr Cooper exchanged impressed looks. 'I'm very familiar with Mr King and his late father's work. They're well-respected engineers whose innovations are legendary.'

'Jasper King, the son of the founder, was instrumental in establishing my involvement in the Baltimore Southern. He's also my brother-in-law. If you'd like, I can arrange for you to meet him and he'll vouch for me, my trustworthiness and the solidity of the Baltimore Southern Railway.'

'Yes, I'd like that very much.' Not since

Silas had first offered praise and appreciation of Mr Williams's designs at the beginning of their meeting had Mr Williams's eyes been so wide.

'Then name the establishment where we'll meet, somewhere more conducive to a business conversation than our present accommodations, and I'll arrange it at once.'

It took Mr Williams a mere second to come up with a name, one that almost made Silas's wallet hurt, except in matters of business he refused to be frugal or to wince at spending. That was for the grocer's bills and menial household expenses. 'I've never dined at Rules. I understand their roast beef is some of the finest in England.'

'Rules it is.' Silas rose to his feet and extended his hand across the table. 'I look forward to our dinner.'

Outside, Silas tapped on his hat and walked off down the pavement, swinging his walking stick in time to his gait. While Silas had been meeting with Mr Williams, clouds had settled over town, but the darkness of the afternoon did nothing to dampen Silas's mood. Despite the difficulties with Mr Edwards and his mother this morning, his time with Mary and this meeting reminded him of the difference between the boy who'd last walked these streets and the man striding down them today. He'd been lost then, full of energy with nowhere to direct it, his ambitions curtailed by the situation fate had placed him in. Today, he had purpose, position and a confidence that boy had lacked and it would see him through this business deal and whatever challenges at home and the Foundation awaited him. This was who Silas was and everything he'd longed to become, someone who made things happen and pushed through every setback to get the results he craved. He wished Mary was here so he could share his elation with her and all his plans for the Baltimore Southern once he had the patent. She would be thrilled in a way no one here had ever been about his plans and ideas. Silas whistled as he walked, London, for the first time ever, a place of opportunity instead of frustration and loss.

Chapter Twelve

'Hello, my darling wife.' Silas picked Mary up by the waist and spun her around, making her laugh as she held on tight to his shoulders. Her laughter rang out against the walls of the front sitting room where he'd found her when he'd come home. He set her back on her feet, keeping his arms around her waist as he peered down at her. Outside, the clouds and the winter sun added to the darkness, but inside a cheery fire brightened the room. For a moment, Silas pictured her in his Baltimore house greeting him in his splendid sitting room with the same anticipation and excitement she held right now. The feeling hit him so strongly it left him without words until she broke the silence.

'All went well with Mr Williams? He gave you the patent?'

'Not yet, but he will. I must write to Richard about it at once.' He tried to release her to go to the desk and pen a letter of his progress to Richard and to enquire as to how their friend was doing, but Mary held tight to his arms, keeping him close.

'Your correspondence can wait.'

'Yes, it can.' In his enthusiasm, he'd almost forgotten the little stop between Mr Williams's and here. 'I have a present for you to celebrate my—I mean our impending victory.'

He withdrew a slim velvet box from his inner coat pocket and held it out to her. She gasped when he opened it to reveal a strand of pearls. It delighted him to see her take as much joy in his success as she did his gift.

She held them up, admiring the creamy roundness of the orbs that reflected the firelight. 'You shouldn't have.'

'But I did.' He had selected and purchased the gift, not Tibbs.

'I'm glad you did. I love them.' She fastened the pearls around her neck, then hurried to the mirror over the fireplace to admire them. He came up behind her, slowly turning her to face him. He bent down and kissed her, savouring the taste of her mouth and her body pressed tight to his. This enthusiasm and acceptance was everything he'd always wanted when he'd lived here and it was finally his. He longed to carry her upstairs and be alone, the two of them together in their belief in each other and their future.

Tibbs clearing his throat in the doorway made them break apart. Silas slipped off his hat and overcoat and handed them to the valet, who carried the garments off to be brushed and hung. He'd forgotten how sooty the air of London was. Baltimore had its moments of bad air, but nothing like this old city. 'And what did you do this afternoon?'

'I helped your mother teach the Foundation women to sew.'

'And?'

'It went a great deal better than I expected. Your mother has a way with those women, all women who've been in their situation.' She fiddled with his lapel, not meeting his eyes.

'What did you expect?'

'That she'd ask me to pack my things and leave, especially after her cool welcome.'

'I told you that's how she is with everyone

who comes here.' Clearly, Mary hadn't believed it.

'But working with fallen women is one thing. Having your son marry one is entirely different.'

'Remember what I told you before.'

'I'm not a fallen woman, but a prosperous businessman's wife.'

He took her hands and clasped them in his large ones, holding them against his chest. 'Any time you are in danger of forgetting that, you come to me and I'll remind you.'

'I promise, I will.'

The jingle of equipage for a carriage stopping outside the doors drifted into the room. The sheer size of the vehicle coming to a stop in front of the Fairclough home dampened the already dark light at the window.

'Who could that be?' Silas wondered.

'A Foundation patroness, perhaps? The carriage is too fine for anyone else.'

Silas moved aside the window curtain to have a look, Mary pushing in beside him to see.

'It's Millie, arriving like a queen!' Silas hurried out into the hallway to throw open the door and greet his sister, stopping at the sight of her. Like Mary, she'd abandoned the plain dark dresses he remembered her wearing for a chic silk gown, her hair done up in ringlets by a talented hand instead of the simple chignon she used to wear. A fine set of gold earrings dangled from her ears, but the smile she offered him reminded him that beneath all the finery was the twin sister he remembered.

'Silas!' Millie threw herself into his arms and gave him a hearty hug. Then she leaned back to take him in as much as he did her before both of them burst out in laughter. 'What a couple of peacocks we've become.'

'The look suits us very well.'

'You perhaps better than me, this is what you always wanted.'

'And I'm not disappointed, especially in you. Imagine, my sister a marchioness.' He raised her hand over her head and spun her around, making her expensive silk skirt flare out around her.

'Sometimes I can barely wrap my head around it, especially since everything has happened so fast, and now you're married and to an earl's daughter of all people.'

'I see Lottie didn't waste any time telling you about my wife.'

'She was at my house the moment she left yours. If all the business of being a marchioness hadn't kept me away I'd have been here sooner. Whoever called a lady of the manor a lady of leisure should be horsewhipped. Leisure is not the best word to describe it.'

'All those menus won't write themselves.'

Millie swatted playfully at Silas. 'There's a great deal more to it than menus. So many people on Cassius's estate and in his Grosvenor Square house rely on us for help, advice or medicine when they or a loved one is sick. At times it's like working here again and I'm glad. I want to be useful.'

'You will be, more so than any other Marchioness of Falconmore before you, I'm only sorry I wasn't here for the wedding.' Silas escorted her into the sitting room where Mary waited for them. 'Or you in America to see my wedding. Millie, this is my wife, Lady Mary.'

'How wonderful to meet you!' Millie clasped Mary in a tight hug before holding her out at arm's length. 'I have so many questions for you.'

'For me?' The reservation that had marked so much of Mary's manner whenever they were in the house came over her again. He wondered what it was about Millie that made her uncomfortable. Millie was nothing like the other women of the class she'd joined and she never would be. All the titles, lands and jewellery might enhance her, but it would never change her. She was too confident in herself and who she was to allow it.

'I'm forever choosing the wrong dish at dinner or irritating my lady's maid by doing something myself. I need someone who can tell me how to do it all without looking down on me because I wasn't born to it.'

'I'd be happy to help you,' Mary said with a smile that was more forced than natural. 'It's a great deal to remember even if you are born to it.'

'It is, but now I have a sister to help me through it.' Millie linked her arm in Mary's and guided her to the sofa. It touched Silas to see his sister who had been raised so high easily accept Mary, but there was no mistaking the tension in Mary's posture. 'And congratulations on the birth of your nephew. Your sister and parents must be so happy.'

'I imagine they are,' Mary mumbled through a weak smile.

The news about Mary's family shocked Silas as much as Millie's change in station. Mary rarely spoke of her family, but it seemed to him the announcement of a new member was something to share. He wondered why she hadn't mentioned it, but he couldn't ask as Millie cornered Mary in conversation, peppering her with questions about the wedding and her and Silas's time together before moving on to how to deal with difficult housekeepers and what dances and foods were appropriate for a wedding ball.

Mary's stiff shoulders relaxed as the conversation flowed, her rigid smile softening into one of genuine enjoyment as she explained the difference between the courses and what to serve when. It gave Silas hope that whatever had troubled her at the start of this meeting was gone, never to bother them again.

Mary sat across from Silas's sister, enjoying the ability to share with someone who didn't look down on her everything she'd learned growing up, to help a woman as genuinely nice and kind as Millie to navigate a world Mary knew could be very harsh. However, it didn't relieve the worry that had gripped her ever since Silas had recognised the woman stepping out of the carriage. Millie was friendly and grateful for Mary's help and guidance but what would happen when she went home and told the Marquess about Mary or when Silas tried to take her to his house? Mary wasn't foolish enough to believe that endearing herself to Millie would be enough to secure her acceptance in the Marquess of Falconmore's household or shield her or Millie from the criticism that was sure to come once people learned that the disgraced Earl of Ashford's daughter was polluting Grosvenor Square.

'You'll be at the wedding ball, won't you?' Millie asked.

'It's hard to picture you at a ball, much less hosting one.' Silas laughed with an exuberance that Mary didn't share. All she experienced was dread. 'Look at you, you'd put the Duchess of Devonshire to shame.'

'If it weren't for the help of my wonderful lady's maid and now you, Mary, I'd put my husband to shame. Tell me you'll both be there.'

'Of course, we wouldn't miss the ball for anything, would we, Mary?' Silas responded, laying his arm around her shoulder and giving her a hearty squeeze.

The desire to flee out of the house and take refuge in Westminster Abbey and never come out, as if she were some sort of medieval criminal, stole over Mary, but she forced herself to remain by Silas's side with a wide smile on her lips, afraid he might guess at some of the terror coursing through her. Silas was always so brave in the face of any challenge, from asking men for money to being quite sure he would receive the patent to the new steam engine. Mary wished she had his confidence, especially today.

'No, we won't miss it,' Mary half-heartedly answered, already concocting a number of excuses she could employ to make sure she did not attend that ball. Just as she knew how to plan a menu, she knew the damage her presence could do to the new Marchioness and her family and she could not inflict that on them. She hated to act the coward, it's what Preston had been, but she couldn't face the Falcon-mores and have the Marquess stare down his nose at her or banish her from his house and his wife's life, refusing to soil his good name with the likes of her. She didn't wish to endure again the look that she'd seen on her father's and her brother's faces that last fateful day that they'd been together.

'Why didn't you mention that you had a sister and a nephew?' Silas asked once they were alone together in their room, dressing for dinner. Millie had stayed for over two hours, peppering Mary with questions about the proper protocol for the ball, including the dressing and placement of footmen and how to hold a receiving line, but obligations at her husband's home had forced her to leave before dinner, much to her and, surprisingly, Mary's disappointment. Mary liked Millie as much as she did Lottie, enjoying the life and energy they brought to the house. Foxcomb Hall or her family's Mayfair town house had never been so cheerful, even when she and her brother and sister had been children. There had been too much minding of manners, keeping out from underfoot, rules and strictures for the manor to have the joy this simple house in this questionable part of London did whenever Silas and his siblings were together.

They are my family now, too.

Or at least they were for the moment, until her past forced Millie and her husband to turn their backs on her.

Mary fiddled with her earring, the fastener on it biting into the delicate skin of her earlobe, Silas's question as much as reality weighing her down. 'Like your sister, I read about it in the newspaper this morning. No one told me because, unlike your sisters, my sister shouldn't be writing to me and my brother wanted nothing more to do with me after it all happened. It's why Ruth and Richard are so important to me. For the last few years, they're all I've had. I don't talk about my family because what can I say? They turned their backs on me, except for my sister, Jane, but she is so limited in what she can do.'

'I'm sorry. I didn't know.' He twisted the signet ring on his finger. 'Maybe you could find some way to see her and your nephew while you're here.'

'I can't. Her husband wouldn't allow it.' She paced the room, anxious at the idea of reaching out to Jane. 'I knew the Longfords. They lived close to us and we went to their house and they came to ours many times. Charitable and forgiving are not words I would use to describe any of them. Jane doesn't need to have her in-laws or my parents come down on her for daring to defy my father to write to me and I don't want to lose the one person in my family who didn't forget me. If anything should happen to you like it happened to Ruth, and if Richard is gone then, I don't want to be entirely alone.'

Tears of fear clouded her vision and she did all she could to hold them back. She wanted to be brave like him, but the news of Jane and the fears of Lord Falconmore made it difficult.

'Nothing is going to happen to me and you have my family. You will never be alone.' He wrapped his arms around her and caressed her back. She clung to him, her tears wetting the wool of his suit. In the past she'd been ashamed of her tears and the self-pity and regret that echoed in every one of them. Alone with him she allowed them to flow. He didn't look down on her for crying, but continued to hold and comfort her. She rested her head on his chest and listened to the steady beat of his heart beneath her ear. In the circle of his arms the distance from her family didn't feel as all-consuming and the loneliness it had created in her life faded away.

Silas laid his cheek on the top of Mary's head as he gently rocked her, her pain his. Her family hadn't forgiven her for her transgression, neither had his mother forgiven his given the tension over the last two days, but she and his sisters hadn't cut him from their lives either, even if they'd had every right to after the way he'd slunk away. He'd been able to return home and, if he trod carefully around his mother, he might find some kind of reconciliation. Mary wasn't likely to have a chance at either. 'Don't worry, Mary. All will be well. I promise.'

She leaned back in his arms to look at him. 'How can you always be so sure?'

'Because I refuse to allow it to be any other way.' He cupped her face with his hands, amazed how in so short a time her life had become so deeply interwoven with his, that she should mean as much to him as the people residing in this house and that he should crave her happiness and safety as much as he did theirs. It pained him to see her hurt and suffer the way he had. She didn't deserve it and he would do everything he could to banish it, to make her happy and to hold her through these heartaches. They were husband and wife, for better or for worse.

He touched his lips to hers, a tender kiss not of passion but of the warmth and growing affection. He was a part of her life and she his and together they would muddle their way through these heartaches and make better, happier memories, and a family of their own.

Chapter Thirteen

'Slowly, I don't want you to twist an ankle in the dark.' Silas held tight to Mary's hand as they tiptoed through the hallways of the Fairclough house and into the Foundation building next door. They'd spent their time after dinner together whiling away the hours until the noises outside had quieted and the light beneath his mother's door had finally gone out.

Together they crept through the Foundation's dark hallways, pausing now and again whenever they thought they heard footsteps overhead, but there were no sounds except a cat crying on the street outside. Everyone was asleep and Silas prayed Mr Edwards was, too. His heart pounded as fiercely as it had when he'd climbed aboard the ship in Liverpool, aware that once they cast off, he couldn't change his mind and turn back. If anyone caught him and Mary here, he had no good explanation for why they were skulking about, at least not one his mother would believe. She'd be disappointed in him once again.

'Not much further. It's just there at the end of the hall,' Silas whispered, trying to hold back the laugh of nervousness gripping them both. They were adults sneaking through the house like a couple of wayward children making for the kitchen to steal a tart. Except if Silas was caught, the distance between him and his mother would grow wider than he feared it already was. She'd asked him not to pry into the Foundation books and he was going behind her back and ignoring her dictates. It was almost enough to make him demand that they turned around, but he continued leading Mary down the hall. He was doing this for his mother and the Foundation. Even if she couldn't see it, it was the truth.

'Here we are.' He pushed open the door and waved Mary inside. Silas followed her, carefully closing the door behind him so as not to make any noise.

'Where should we begin?' Mary whispered

as Silas lit the lamp and turned it up as little as he dared while still allowing them to see. If anyone came down the hall, they'd notice the light under the door and they would be caught.

'Let's see what he keeps in this office. Look for any of my letters or bank drafts, anything that might be out of the ordinary, but make sure you don't disturb too much. I don't want him to notice anything amiss.'

He and Mary picked through the letters, papers and correspondence on the desk and in the drawers, careful not to leave it all out of sorts. They found nothing.

'Now what?' Mary asked.

'The ledgers.' Silas sat at the desk and flipped open the book, aware that only this month and last month's were in the office. Who knew where the manager kept the others? Silas hoped that if there was any evidence to be found, it was here or that Mr Edwards hadn't taken advantage of Silas's delay to erase it.

'What are you looking for?' Mary leaned over his shoulder, the lavender scent of her enticing in the tight confines of the room. He'd rather be with her upstairs in his bed than here, but this had to be done, even if guilt plagued him while he did it. Despite his earlier protests, he was accusing a potentially innocent man of misdeeds.

'I'm not sure, but I've seen enough books in my time to recognise discrepancies.'

'What should I do?'

'Sit by the door and listen in case anyone is up so we can douse the lamp as quickly as possible.'

Mary sat in the slender chair beside the door, diligent in her guard duties while Silas studied the ledger. Page after page he reviewed the figures, waiting for something to reveal itself even if he wasn't sure what it might be.

It felt like hours went by before he closed the current ledger and reached for last month's. Beside him on the desk, the lamp flame flickered, the oil inside the well running low. Silas hoped there was enough left for it to burn until at least before sunrise even if sunrise seemed like ages away, though it could be minutes, he couldn't tell. The night had stretched on far longer than he'd imagined a night could, except the one his father had died. Time had almost stood still then, but the grief that had haunted him in that darkness hung over his shoulder like the chill in the house. This was what his father had always hoped he would do, what his parents had expected of him, what he'd failed to do until a crisis had forced him back to it.

'The oil in the lamp is almost gone.' Mary's quiet voice broke the still. 'You can't work in the dark.'

'I know.' Silas set down his pencil and sat up, rubbing the stiffness out of his back, but he made no move to refill the lamp, almost praying it would go out and end this night of clandestine work. He was no closer to finding any answers about the missing money or giving himself a legitimate reason for defying his mother and risking more of her disappointment. There was nothing out of sorts with the ledger entries, no hint that his money had been here before it'd been squirrelled away to somewhere else, its existence hidden in an improperly added sum or an erased figure or some outlandish grocer bill that had been forged. Either Silas had failed to notice any suspicious entries or there were none to be found.

Without being asked, Mary lit a candle and placed it beside the oil lamp, then blew out the wick, casting the small office into a darkness

broken only by the orange flicker of the flame.
She slid off the hurricane glass with a delicate
grip, her movements fluid, easy, untouched
by the tension inside Silas. Then she refilled
the lamp, the oil smell a harsh contrast to her
fresh scent. With the scrape of the thin glass
against its metal base, she replaced the glass
and lit the wick. Light filled the room again
and she set the lamp on the desk.

'Thank you.' He wasn't sure he should. He
appreciated her gentle care, but not the harsh-
ness of the light or the figures in front of him.
He used to work on these books with Septimus
while longing to escape the grind of it and here
he was sneaking in to do it again. The irony
was not lost on him.

'Anything?' Mary whispered when Silas finally reached the last page of the last ledger,
then closed it.

'Nothing. It all appears in order. My mother
was right.' He shouldn't have questioned her or
been so quick to spark what could have been a
nasty argument, the kind that would have made
everything that his quick departure from England
years ago had already made even worse.

She laid her hands on his shoulders and

rubbed out the stiffness that had settled there. 'Be glad it isn't Mr Edwards. There'll be a great deal less trouble between you and your mother because of it.'

'You're right.' He laid his hands over the tops of hers. 'I suppose I was looking for the easy answer.'

'Perhaps you'll learn something when you visit the bank today.'

'I hope so. I don't want to fail my mother and the Foundation again.'

Mary knelt before him and rested her hands on his knees. 'You aren't a failure, you never have been, but a man who strives and carries on in the face of whatever difficulties he's facing.'

Silas caressed her face, bolstered by her faith in him. He would meet this new challenge as he had all the ones before and he would prevail. He had to or his conscience would burden him even more than it already did.

'Sir, all of the bank drafts were cashed,' Mr Perkins, the slender bank manager with the slicked-back brown hair, told Silas from across the mahogany desk in his office. Outside, the sounds of shuffling shoes and the murmur of conversation as people deposited and withdrew fund from their accounts filled the air. Silas fought his exhaustion from the night spent perusing the Foundation books with Mary to concentrate on what the man had said.

'That can't be. My family never received any of the money I sent,' Silas insisted, irritated at arriving at what appeared to be another frustratingly dead end. 'Who cashed them?'

The manager opened the leather folio in front of him and flipped through the stack of papers inside before selecting one and laying it on top and then turning the folder around so Silas could read it. There in black and white were the cashed bank drafts, all of them signed by Tom Smith on behalf of the Foundation.

'No one by this name was authorised to cash those drafts.'

'According to this letter, he is.' The clerk showed him a letter with Silas's signature at the bottom authorising this Tom, whoever he was, to collect the funds on behalf of the Foundation. He leaned back in his chair as if to say the matter was resolved and no longer his concern.

Silas read the letter written in a hand he didn't recognise, but there at the bottom was his signature. It wasn't unusual for him to dictate letters to Mr Hachman and then sign them, but he had never asked for or sent this one and this was not written in Mr Hachman's hand.

'This is a forgery.'

'How can you be certain, Mr Fairclough? Perhaps, given the time it takes for letters to reach England, it was simply overlooked or forgotten.'

'I know it is forgery because I gave instructions to this bank that a letter from me and my English solicitor is required for any changes to the management of the money. Given my residence in America, it's meant as a safeguard against exactly this kind of situation.' Silas rasped his knuckles against the desk, furious that the protocol he'd established to prevent something like this had been ignored. If he'd been here in England, it wouldn't have been necessary, but he wouldn't have had the money to make this account and the personalised attention he was receiving from the bank manager either. 'When Septimus Clark retired, you received the double correspondence allowing the new manager to cash the drafts. Why wasn't it done this time?'

The manager flipped through the folio, Silas guessed, in search of the letter from the solicitor but, as expected, there was none. 'Unless this forger was clever enough to create two letters, you will not find the authorising letter from my solicitor.'

'No, it does not appear to be here,' the manager mumbled, his confidence in his institution and his doubts about Silas's claim of the bank mishandling his account gone. The manager's face went red and he assumed a much more conciliatory posture than when Silas had first began discussing the issue with him. 'I apologise, sir, but in the last few months we have merged with another institution and I'm sorry to say that this isn't the first mistake we've caught as clerks familiar with some accounts have been let go and new ones hired. I'm afraid your account and the instructions pertaining to it were caught in the confusion and failed to come to our attention in a timely manner.'

There was no accusation in the man's profuse apology and explanation, but Silas couldn't help but hear one. Silas hadn't been here to notice trouble or to stop it before it had threatened to put the Foundation and his family at risk. All he could do was try to clean up the mess his absence had helped create and even in this he was barely succeeding. 'I wish to speak to the clerk who regularly processed these transactions. I want to know what the man who did this looks like.' It was the only lead Silas had as to the forger's identity.

'I'm afraid that clerk is on holiday, but he's set to return soon. Once he does, we'll pay you a visit to discuss the matter further. In the meantime, I'll do all I can to ensure that nothing like this ever happens again. We value your faith in us and your business and we would hate to have it ruined by this unfortunate matter.'

Silas's faith in this bank was already gone and he would find a new institution to handle his English affairs once the forger was found. However, for the moment he merely offered the manager his thanks. If Silas announced that he was going to move the account, the manager might wash his hands of the matter quicker than he'd been about to do until he'd realised his bank's role in this incident, then Silas would never get a good description of the man who'd forged his signature or recover the missing funds.

* * *

Silas watched the train engine roar through the London and Greenwich Railway station near London Bridge, the rush of wind against him offering a momentary relief from the barrage of thoughts tumbling through his mind. It'd been years since he'd last sat here, when this had been the only place in London where he'd been able to find any kind of calm. It was Mary by his side, her small hand pressed into his, that brought him the most comfort tonight.

'It has to be someone familiar with the family, the signature on the letter was an exact copy of mine. Also, all the letters I've sent home that would've alerted people to the fact that the money was being stolen have gone missing, too, and I received none of their letters to me. It must be someone in the Foundation who had access to our correspondence.'

'After all your mother has done for them, how could anyone there betray her like this?'

'One or two in the past have repaid our generosity by betraying our trust, but it was usually obvious fairly soon or they did not stay around long enough to do this kind of damage.'

'Maybe your mother will have an inkling of who might be involved?'

Silas titled his head back in frustration, anticipating the hundred more problems emerging from this little twist. 'If I ask my mother about the women, she'll think I'm second-guessing her judgement or throwing scorn on women who've received enough for a lifetime, especially if I'm wrong about their involvement with the forger.'

He touched his signet ring, practically able to hear his father reminding him that he hadn't been raised to look down on fallen women and that his time grasping after money had made him suspicious of some of the most vulnerable people. His father was no longer here to say those words, but his mother was and he refused to hear them for the second time. The sound of them after he'd spoken to Mr Edwards about the ledgers had been enough.

'Then wait until the clerk returns and provides a description. It'll give you more evidence and, in the end, maybe you won't have to question her.'

'I don't like sitting still when there's something to be done.'

'You must until you have more evidence or it might make things worse.'

'I know.' He wrapped his arm around her shoulders and pressed a kiss to her temple. She smelled of rosewater perfume and the faint soot of passing trains. The burning coal from the smokestacks left small flecks of ash on the thick pelisse she wore over her fine dress. He didn't want his wife sitting in the grime of the city, but in the splendour and grace to which she'd been born and to which her marriage to him had raised her again, but he'd needed to come here, away from the Foundation, to think. 'Let's be off. A little shopping, perhaps, a new pair of gloves or a fine fan for you to carry to Millie's wedding celebration. I want you to turn every head and make every woman jealous of you. I also want you to work on Millie about coming to America, give her a woman's view of it while I convince the Marquess to make the journey. I don't know what kind of man he is, but if Millie married him, he can't be all bad. He could add a great deal of aristocratic glamour to the Baltimore Southern.'

He tugged Mary off the bench, ready to lead her to the somewhat cleaner air of Jermyn Street. He wanted them both to return to America more polished than when they'd left and for Mary to set the fashion in Baltimore instead of following it. Silas was stunned when Mary pulled out of his grip and he turned to face her, baffled by the sight of her hands balled in fists at her sides and the hard set of her lips.

'You'll have to win over the Marquess and your sister without me. I can't go to the ball.'

'What do you mean? Of course you can go.'

'I can't and I won't.' Mary hated how the fear undermined her. She should be there helping Silas the way she'd promised to do when she'd become his wife, when she'd sold herself to him as a solid investment worthy of his name and his future, but she couldn't. Her past made it impossible. 'I don't know who might be there and what they might say to either me, society or your sister if they see me.'

'I don't care what they say. They mean nothing to us.'

'They mean something to your sister and to the Foundation. If word of my being in England and my now-intimate connection to the Foundation gets around, then the donors your mother relies on to fund her work might abandon her. I refuse to create more need simply to peacock in front of people who won't care what I am wearing or that I'm married because I'm already tarnished goods in their eyes.'

'I don't care about their opinions and neither should you. As for the Foundation, with the Baltimore Southern, the foundry and the new engine, I'll have enough money so my mother never has to rely on donations again.'

'But what about Millie? Society will scorn her when they realise I'm related to her by marriage. Things must be difficult enough for her already because she's an outsider. My being a fallen woman with a reputation will make it even worse.'

'Millie has dealt with far worse things than a few old matrons looking askance at her and she can handle this.' Silas stepped up to her, taking her by the arms and making her face him. 'It's you who has to stop referring to yourself like you're no better than a gutter rat. You're not that woman any more. That time is behind you.'

'It will never be behind me, not in England.

You didn't grow up in that world. You don't realise how cruel it can to be. You've been in America where a man who pulls himself up by the bootstraps is admired by other men, fêted and cheered. Here they'll look down on your achievements, even more so because of me, and I don't know what kind of repercussions that will have for you and your family.'

'There won't be any repercussions because I won't allow them. The men I deal with in business don't care about the goings on of the hoi polloi and neither do I.'

She shook out of his grasp, frustrated at his unwillingness to see the truth. 'You can't control this like you do your railroad.'

'And you can't allow others' opinions to dominate you.'

'Don't dismiss my concerns as if they're nothing when you know better. Your father lost contact with his father because of what he chose to do just like I lost contact with mine when I did the same. The consequences of our actions are real, no matter how much you attempt to ignore them.'

'They're only real if you let them be real. Those people can only judge you if you let them. If you come to the ball and show them that they can't harm you, that their opinions mean nothing to you, that you have succeeded despite all of their attempts to humiliate and dismiss you, then you will win.'

'It isn't about winning or losing or pretending that their scorn isn't real because it is, you simply haven't felt it hard enough to realise it and I can't have that.' She couldn't risk him or his family facing the full brunt of society's disapproval and have him turn away from her in disgust the way Preston had, to look at her not as he did now as a woman of possibility and worth, but as a damaged one who had dragged him down into the mire with her. She couldn't do that to him, not after everything he'd done for her. 'Don't pretend that we can change the minds of London society through determination. We can't, any more than you can make this bank-draft affair clear up simply by insisting it be done or force your mother to see your side of things. Not every problem can be overcome by willing yourself to overcome it.'

Silas stood in the middle of the train platform, staring at Mary, at a loss for words. He couldn't force her to go to the ball, not with the anguish marring her face and the irrefutable facts she'd thrown at him, but the resignation swathing her was more than he could bear, especially since everything she said was true. Not every problem could be willed away or pushed through. Some could never be overcome as he'd discovered the night his father had died. Nothing he did, no words he uttered or belief in himself or his ability to succeed, could ever give him the few moments he'd needed with his father to ask for his forgiveness, to assure him that he did love him and that his loss was more than he could bear.

No, that opportunity might have passed him by, but it didn't mean every other trouble was a lost cause. 'There's always a solution for every problem, a way to work around any difficulty, even this. One simply has to find it.'

'There is and it's my not going to the wedding ball.'

'I don't accept that.'

'You don't have a choice.' Mary marched past him and out of the station. Silas followed silently behind her before catching up to walk by her side.

'I won't let you give up, Mary.'

'I'm not going to the ball, Silas. Maybe you can't see it now, but eventually you'll see the wisdom behind that decision.'

Surrender wasn't his habit and that's what she was doing, surrendering to what others wanted of her, to their vision of her and her life, and he refused to allow it. 'What I see is a woman giving in to her fears.'

Mary jerked to a stop to face him, a fire burning in her eyes she'd never turned on him before and it wasn't one of determination. 'Don't you dare call me a coward, not after everything I've been through, everything I've endured. They all tried to crush me and they didn't, but it doesn't mean I have to subject myself to more of their hate and venom. No person, not even you, is capable of bearing that much derision.'

She whirled around and marched off down the street, storming past hawkers and other people enjoying the last of the cloudless but cold winter day. Silas wanted to turn around in disgust and walk back to the train station, to sit and watch the steam engines hurling down the tracks while he thought of a thousand rea-

sons why she was wrong, a hundred ways he
could convince her that this could all be overcome, but he didn't move.

Failure crept over him like the coming evening darkness. He'd been naive to believe he
could banish her fears, reservations and heartache about being home simply by reminding
her that she was no longer her past. He'd been
too enraptured by the idea of their future together to realise how much her mistakes truly
haunted her the same way his bothered him.
He didn't want her to dwell in it—he knew
the danger of residing in old hurts and regret,
he'd spent the years since his father's death
and his escape to America doing that—but he
also knew one couldn't be forced to shrug off
blame and sorrow. One simple had to bear it.

Silas walked slowly towards home, stay-
ing far enough behind Mary to keep her in
his sights and make sure that she was safe,
but giving them both some time alone. What
she'd said was right. He'd tried to dismiss her
past with flippant words about it not matter-
ing and that the future was the only thing she
should concentrate on. He wouldn't have appreciated it if she'd told him that what had

happened with his father and then his mother didn't matter and that he should simply dismiss it. Her wounds, like his, were too deep to just set aside. In America, they could be ignored, but not here where her ghosts and his were too present and real. All he could do was protect her as much as he could, to shield her from the malicious tongues and opinions of others instead of forcing her to endure them, even if giving in to the petty will of others felt like capitulation at a time when he wanted to fight.

When they reached the busy corner, he caught up to her with quick strides. She didn't look at him, but kept walking straight ahead.

'You don't have to attend the ball. I'll make your excuses to Mother and Millie.' The words rolled across his tongue like the pit of a cherry. He hated to say them, but he couldn't force her to go, to face all those biddies who felt themselves morally superior because they trod on women who were already down and tried to kick them back in the gutter when they dared to step out of it to better themselves. The thought of not having her by his side stung. He'd wanted to show her off and help instil in her more of the confidence she'd shown at the head of Richard's table and at the Christmas-time Ball, the confidence that failed her in the gloom and fog of London.

'Thank you.' She didn't take his arm, but walked beside him as they made their way home, a strange quiet settling between them. She was next to him and yet he felt the distance. He wanted to reach out to her, but he couldn't, not tonight. All his prior assurances and promises had failed to make her realise that she was more than her past and more than what people here wanted her to be.

He wondered if she blamed him for her current heartache, for his having wanted her to return to England instead of remaining behind. That she'd chosen to come at Richard's urging didn't ease his guilt. Silas had been the one who'd arranged for her passage originally, who'd concocted this idea that she join him, forcing this heartache on her the way his having cowardly fled England years ago had forced heartache on his mother. He wasn't sure how he'd make this right, but he would find a way.

Mary stood over the young woman seated at the Foundation's dining table and corrected the way she held the needle. 'Like this. It will make your stitches more even.'

'Thank you, Lady Mary,' the girl said before scrunching her face in concentration as she executed a few more stitches, all them more even than the last.

'There, that's much better.'

It was the second week of February and Mary had spent most of today, as she had the last few days, helping the Foundation women while Silas met with Jasper King to arrange their dinner with Mr Williams and discuss how they would win him over. She was glad he was thinking of something other than her and Millie's wedding ball tonight. After they'd come home from the train station last week, the subject had not been broached again, but it had hung unspoken between them throughout dinner and afterwards when they had lain in bed together, each of them far off in their own thoughts. She hadn't asked Silas what his were. Hers were still torturing her. Thankfully, the business of reviewing new steam inventions at the Royal Society had occupied his time the last few days while lectures by prominent engineers meant he'd come home long after she'd retired for the night.

Mary continued around the table to inspect the other women's sewing, trying to concentrate on them and not the words she'd flung at Silas at the train station. She enjoyed this work and the time she'd spent here with the women over the last week, but it wasn't enough to calm her worries about the lingering tension between her and her husband. Mary had told Silas to continue being brave in the face of the setbacks with the money and Mr Williams while Mary ran in fear from her ghosts. She was allowing the past to make her ashamed of herself instead of believing in who she was the way Silas always encouraged. He'd been doing all he could to raise up her opinion of herself and all she'd done was tear him down for his efforts, the way her father used to tear down her mother whenever she'd show even a little spirit. It wasn't kind of her, but she'd had to make him see why she could not go to the ball tonight. He had, but still it left her feeling no better. She was the coward he'd accused her of being, afraid to show her face in society for fear of what people who no longer mattered to her, who would never be in her life again once she and Silas returned to Baltimore, might say to her. She should face them and fling their derision right back in their faces, but she couldn't. It wasn't only her they would attack if she dared to walk among them with even a tenth of the pride Silas had tried to instil in her, there was also Silas's family. Maybe he couldn't see the way she was trying to protect him and his sisters, but she could and that's what had made his inability to understand her concerns hurt all the more.

She rounded the table to look at another young woman's work and give her some guidance on her stitches. The clock on the mantel at the far end of the room chimed five times and the women set down their sewing with a mixture of relief and disappointment depending on their skill with the needle and how much they truly enjoyed the task. As they filed out of the room to help prepare the dinner in the kitchen, Mary cleaned up the scraps of fabric and carefully arranged any errant spools of thread or envelopes of needles in the sewing boxes, anything to avoid going next door to face the fact that she was not dressing for the ball. Lilian was already upstairs doing her hair in anticipation of tonight, having accepted

Silas and Mary's excuse for Mary not attending without question or comment.

When the dining room was finally tidied and there was nothing left to keep Mary here, she made her way back to the Fairclough home. Silas wasn't there, having sent word for Tibbs to deliver his evening clothes to Mr King's house where Silas would dress before coming here in a hired carriage to collect his mother and go to the ball. For Mary it would be a quiet evening at home like the many others she'd endured over the last four years.

It'll all be different when we're back home.

There would be balls and dinners, some of them hosted in her and Silas's home.

'Mary, would you mind helping me dress?' Lilian asked when Mary reached the top of the stairs, before she could slip into the solitude of her and Silas's bedroom where her blue ball gown, the one the modiste in Baltimore had made for her, hung limp and unused in the wardrobe.

'Of course.' Mary wondered what Lilian needed help with. The maid had arranged her wavy dark brown hair into fetching ringlets appropriate for her age. Her gown was a deep crimson shot with silver thread. It was of an older style, but it flattered her slender figure and softened the mature angles of her face.

Mary was stunned when she entered Lilian's room to find her blue-silk ball gown laid out across the bed.

'I couldn't help but notice the tension between you and Silas this last week,' Lilian said at Mary's look of astonishment. 'And then you not going tonight.'

'Did he explain to you why? The real reason?' Mary fingered her watch, wanting to confess her past so Lilian might better understand but she didn't want this kind woman's face to turn to horror the way Mary's mother had when she'd told her everything.

'He didn't tell me all of it, but I've had enough years of experience with the women here to guess.'

'Then you see why I can't go?'

'I also recognise how important it is that you do.'

Lilian spoke like Richard had when he'd encouraged her to come to England. She'd followed her friend's advice and she still wasn't sure if it had been the right choice. 'I can't. I don't want you or Millie or Silas to suffer for my mistakes.'

'We won't. I called on Millie this afternoon and explained the situation. She and her husband will stand by you.'

'How can you be sure of him?' She had little faith in those of her former class who had disappointed her more than she was disappointing Silas and Lilian tonight.

'Because in the short time that Lord Falconmore has been my son-in-law, I've seen how generous and kind a man he is. He has a great deal of influence that he can use to sway others in your favour or at least blunt their sharp tongues if you're brave enough to face them.' She approached Mary and laid her hands on her shoulders. 'I understand your fears, Mary, but don't allow them to rule your life. Use the advantages you have and rely on the people who care about you to help you. Silas adores you as much as you adore him and you complement each other well. Be by his side tonight, where you belong.'

It was one thing for Richard to ask Mary to face a host of possibilities that might never occur by joining Silas in England. Lilian was asking Mary to risk a near certainty to be with

Silas tonight. In America there might be whispers about her one day but here they would be overt remarks and well-timed cuts. She'd endured them once, she didn't wish to endure them again. She also didn't want to sit home in an empty house in fear and sad regret the way she'd spent so many evenings doing at Ruth's while reading Jane's letters about the life she'd been meant to lead. It didn't have to be like that again. There were people who cared about her who were willing to stand beside her in spite of her past and to help her bear the burden of her mistakes, people like Silas, her husband. She couldn't disappoint him or his family, Richard or herself by giving in to fear. She'd married Silas to reclaim something of her old life and a future and place in the world as his wife. She touched the blue-silk ball gown and imagined what it would be like to walk into Lord Falconmore's house wearing it, a married woman holding her head up high instead of allowing others to define and demean her. There would be whispers and stares, but there would be Silas, too, believing in her in a way very few people ever had before. If he didn't fear her past, if Millie and Lilian didn't fear it either, but were willing to support her and see her redeemed as they had seen a hundred other women who'd once been in her place, then she could summon the courage to face it, too.

Silas paced at the bottom of the stairs, the hired carriage waiting for him and his mother outside. He adjusted the time on his pocket watch, expecting his mother to come down any moment and wishing it was Mary he was about to greet. They'd barely seen each other since their exchange at the railway station. Even when they'd slept together in the same bed, they'd barely touched, each of them too involved in their own troubles to reach out to the other. He should have set aside his concerns and grudges to hold her and comfort her in her worries, but he'd been too involved in mulling over one solution after another, all of which had come to nothing. He wished Richard were here to discuss it with him the way he'd been so many times before, but he wasn't. Mary's concerns were valid and real and he shouldn't have dismissed them so lightly, but once again he'd been too wrapped up in his ambitions to reach out to those he cared for. He was failing

her and it bothered him. He tucked the watch
back in his waistcoat pocket, ready to start for
upstairs to repair the damage he'd allowed to
fester over the last week when the sight at the
top of the landing took his breath away.

Mary stood there in her blue-silk ball gown,
her blonde hair swept up off her neck to reveal
the graceful line of it. The strand of pearls
he'd bought her lay against the smooth skin of
her chest above the beautiful mounds of her
breasts. She glided down the stairs to him like
a dream, her captivating smile drawing him to
her until he held out his hand and she took it to
step into the entryway and join him.

'You're stunning.' She'd changed her mind.
There weren't words to tell her how much it
meant to him and how proud he was of her because of it. She would be beside him tonight,
just as he'd longed for and imagined.

A soft blush spread across her cheeks at his
praise. 'Thank you.'

'Are you sure you wish to go?' He didn't
want to think that he'd somehow forced her
into this decision, that he'd made her do something that would make her unhappy in the end.

She shook her head, her gold earrings shivering like the curls at the back of her head. 'I can't keep running from my past and I'll have you beside me. That's all that matters.'

He laid his hand over hers where it rested in the crook of his arm, determined to live up to her expectations and belief in him and not disappoint her.

Behind her his mother came down the stairs, the small smile turning up the corner of her lips telling him she'd had a part in Mary's change of heart. He whispered 'thank you' over Mary's shoulder and his mother nodded, the pride and happiness in her expression one that he had not seen for a very long time. She loved him even if neither he nor she always had the words to express it. Perhaps there was a chance she would forgive him for what he'd done and through her he could find some peace with what had happened between him and his father. Yet tonight wasn't about regrets or the past, but Millie and Lord Falconmore's life together. With Mary on one arm and his mother on the other, Silas escorted the women to the carriage, eager to arrive at the ball.

Chapter Fourteen

Lord Falconmore's Grosvenor Square house
with its white stucco front, tall columns and
black wrought-iron fence flanking the front
door was awash in light and noise. A flood of
people spilled in from the carriages outside
to promenade up the front walk and enter the
entrance hall that was adorned with a curving
staircase and marble statues tucked in scal-
loped niches in the walls. From somewhere
deep in the house, the high notes of a string
quartet punctuated the chatter and laughter of
the guests while footmen moved silently between the revellers with trays of delicacies and
flutes of champagne.

Mary stood with Silas in the receiving line,
flicking her fan nervously in front of her,
watching every face that went by as they stood

there waiting to greet Silas's sister and her new husband. So far, none of the earth-shattering events that she'd imagined on the carriage ride here had happened. The entire entryway had not fallen silent at the sight of her and no one had pointed and hissed at her in an attempt to drive her out of the house.

Instead, the slights had been more subtle. The eyes of many people she recognised from her past had gone wide at the sight of her and a number of older ladies had ducked behind their fans to whisper and speculate why the fallen daughter of Lord Ashford was at the Marquess of Falconmore's wedding ball. If any of them wondered about Silas, she didn't notice. He meant nothing to them compared to her sudden social resurrection. Every time another jaw dropped at the sight of her, she braced herself, waiting for them to say something or comment overtly. She guessed it was the presence of the lord of the house at the front of the receiving line that kept people from making a scene. She wondered how long his invisible protection would last and how far past this entrance hall it might extend.

'Look at this house,' Silas marvelled as he

craned his neck to take in the frescoes overhead, oblivious to the two of them being the
real centre of attention. 'We'll build one like
this in Baltimore. It'll make even Mr Penniman jealous.'

'No, I want something cosy, a real family
home where children can be themselves, not
some mausoleum.' She tried to match his mood
as she imagined their future abode, to focus on
this and not the gaping people around them,
but it was difficult.

'That'll be our country house,' Silas teased,
eliciting a smile from Mary. 'The one in town
must be designed to impress.'

'We'll have a country house by the seashore
where the children can breathe fresh air.'

'Is there something you're trying to tell me,
Mrs Fairclough?'

'Not at all, I'm only thinking ahead.' His
suggestions shocked her more than Lady Tilt-
bury nearly spilling her champagne when she
caught sight of Mary. Mary did a quick calcu-
lation, Silas's words sparking a thought that
she could not shake. She wished she had a calendar. With all the travel and the distraction
of being in London she'd lost track of when

she'd had her last courses and whether or not they would arrive at any moment or if they were late. A new fear began to creep in under her concerns about the crowd as the receiving line shifted forward, bringing them closer to the Marquess. She was married, she shouldn't be afraid of pregnancy, but the uncertainty of Silas's reaction to a possible child scared her. Preston had abandoned her when she'd needed him most. She clasped Silas's hand tighter. He would never do that to her.

The line moved forward again and Silas and Mary found themselves face to face with the Marquess and Marchioness. Millie exuberantly embraced them both while her husband stood stoically beside her as Millie made the introductions. Mary heard not a word of what she said, waiting for the Marquess to recognise her, to throw her out of his house or look down his very handsome and aristocratic nose at her. She wanted to believe Lilian's assurances that Lord Falconmore would not cut her or demand that she leave while cursing his wife and her brother for daring to bring a shameful woman into his home, but it was hard. She clutched her fan to her chest while she waited, determined to have the same faith in him that Lilian possessed, very aware that she was not the only one waiting for his response. It was as if the entire room had stopped breathing while they watched.

Lord Falconmore didn't order her out of his house or cut her, but bowed to her as she curtsied to him. Either he hadn't heard the story about her and Preston or he didn't care. Mary couldn't say which, but she hoped it was what Lilian had said, that the Falconmores had decided to stand beside her, that some people of her former rank and class had hearts and were worthy of trust and genuine affection.

'Welcome to my home, Lady Mary. Millie tells me you were a great help to her in planning this party,' Lord Falconmore complimented, his piercing blue eyes fixing on Mary with nothing but warmth and welcome. He was tall and well muscled, with a force of presence many of his class did not possess beyond their exalted titles.

'I wouldn't have known where to start in planning the menu if it hadn't been for my new sister-in-law,' Millie announced and Mary clasped Silas harder, fighting the desire to shush Millie, to tell her not to say her name or the family connection so loudly while everyone was still watching.

'Mary is certainly talented.' Silas raised her left hand to his lips and pressed a kiss to the back of it, offering a glimpse of her impressive diamond wedding ring to everyone who was looking. He did it as much to aggrandise them both as to remind her of who she was instead of allowing her to wallow in who she had been. She squeezed his hand tight, glad that he had finally noticed that they were the unofficial centre of the room's attention.

'Not at all, I only offered her some advice. The rest was all Lady Falconmore's doing,' Mary complimented, amazed Lord Falconmore had placed so much credit on her for the magnificence around them. Mary had only offered suggestions and little more, but Millie had taken them to heart and employed them well.

'And she's done a fine job of it.' The Marquess flashed his wife a loving smile, one Mary had never witnessed before between a man of his rank and his wife. All the aristocratic marriages she'd ever seen had been contracted along more practical lines. It was obvious that theirs was the rare love match and she was glad. With Lord Falconmore's love and support Millie could face any of the trials sure to test her during her time as his wife, just as Silas was holding up Mary through hers.

She slid a sideways glance at her husband who spoke to Lord Falconmore, flattering the Marquess as much as possible without coming off as too enamoured. She and Silas might not have gone to the altar in love, but she could feel it building between them, so much so that she did not fear it as she had before nor want to run from it or dismiss it. She wanted to embrace and enjoy it. It had been such a rare thing in her life for far too long.

Restlessness in the line behind them forced them to say their goodbyes to Millie and her Marquess. Silas escorted Mary through the house towards the ballroom at the back, gathering more curious and surprised looks as they went. Mary held her head high as she walked beside him, pretending like Silas did that the amazed people didn't exist, confident in a way she hadn't been in ages.

'Mary, you look gorgeous,' Lottie squealed,

rushing up to her and offering Mary a big hug that caught the notice of the more restrained men and women around them. 'Isn't this grand, all of us here together? Who could have imagined it? Think of what Christmas and all the other holidays will be like with us all together now that you've returned.'

'They won't be here for good, Lottie,' Lilian gently reminded her daughter from where she stood on Silas's other side, she and Lottie seemingly oblivious to how many people were pretending not to watch them.

'But with Mr Cunard's steamships they can come whenever they like. Since Silas has finally returned for the first time, it won't be difficult to persuade him to come again.'

'Or for you to visit us,' Silas countered. 'I can't wait for you and Mother and Millie to see the railway.'

'Neither can I.' Lottie clapped her hands together in glee. 'In the meantime, you must come to dinner at our house. I want you to see it and to dine with us every week while you're here.'

'We wouldn't miss it for anything,' Mary promised, Lottie's enthusiasm, like Silas's, infectious and easing the weight of the room's attention.

'I have to see if Millie has been relieved of her receiving-line duties. I need to remind her that she may be a marchioness, but she's still my sister and not too good to eat at my table. Come, Mother, let's find her.' Lottie took Lilian's arm and pulled her off towards the entry hall where Millie had last been.

Silas and Mary continued on through the house until they reached the large ballroom at the back. Unlike Mrs Penniman's, the ballroom had tall rectangular windows set in fine panelled walls trimmed with gilt and a ceiling of plaster from which hung a number of chandeliers. Mary's newfound confidence threatened to desert her when they stepped into the ballroom and a few couples nearly stumbled at the sight of them. More than one matron's jaw dropped when they spied her before they dipped behind their fans with their friends to speculate if this was really Lord Ashford's daughter brazenly entering a ballroom as if she had every right to be there. It almost made Mary turn and flee until Silas's steadying hand on the small of her back stilled her.

'Ignore them. They don't matter to our lives and soon we'll be in America with a whole ocean between those scowls and us.' It was the first time he'd openly acknowledged that her past was following them as much as the skirt of her dress.

She took in the people watching and whispering about them and something in her rebelled at their scorn. None of them were perfect and she was sure that many of these people had enough family skeletons in their manor closets to make them ashamed of casting aspersions on her. Silas was right. Tonight was simply a moment in what would be a long lifetime in a different country. She refused to allow their disapproving looks to ruin her time with her husband and this small taste of the life she'd once known before she'd been forced to abandon it, except this time she would gladly walk away from it and embrace the future offered to her by Silas and Baltimore.

'Shall we dance?' Silas asked.

'Please.'

He led her out on to the dance floor and took her in his arms for the waltz. This was only the second time they'd danced together, but they moved as if they had been partners for years. If the matrons tutted and scolded, Mary didn't see them, her attention entirely on Silas and his steady lead through the steps, his hand clasped tight to hers, the strength of his legs and his movements as they whirled in unison around the room mesmerising. Her dress rustled in all its silk fineness against the wool of his trousers, his arm firm beneath her gloved palm where she held on tight to him, grateful to be in the circle of his embrace, the troubles of the railway station and the guests watching the dance far behind them.

'I'm glad you decided to come tonight,' Silas said, his breath whispering across her cheeks. 'It means a great deal to me to have you beside me in every endeavour.'

'And for me to be with you. You don't know how much your faith in me means, how different I feel because of it.'

'I have some idea.' He turned them past another couple before their steps led them to the outer circle of dancers and they slipped back into a steady pace. The surety of his lead didn't change, but something in his face did, a seriousness that made him shift closer to her as his grasp on her hand tightened along with the pressure of his fingers on her back. 'You see, I didn't simply leave England five years ago.'

'You don't have to tell me this, not here or tonight.' She hated to break the spell of the dance, but she didn't want to stop him from speaking either. She knew what it was to have the person closest to you hear the truth and pain and make the burden a touch lighter, even if it was only for a little while.

'I want to be honest with you in the way you have always been honest with me.' He flexed his fingers on her back, allowing a few strains of the music to drift between them before he spoke again. 'I didn't simply go to America. I slipped away, leaving behind nothing but the last bit of pay I'd received and a letter explaining where I'd gone. I never said goodbye to anyone and I never told them why I'd left. I didn't think I could or that they'd listen to me even if I did. I was suffocating in Liverpool, aching to get out into the world and make my own way, to create my life as I saw it instead of the way others wanted it to be. I never should have run off.'

'You wouldn't be the man you are today if

you hadn't gone after what you wanted, the way you still do.'

'I was a coward and it wasn't the first time.' The anguish in his face matched the one that had been in her heart when she'd thought of not coming tonight and not being here with Silas. He glanced across the room to where his mother stood with Lottie and Jasper watching the dancers and chatting together. 'I left my father because he didn't understand, I ran off instead of facing him and I never got the chance to apologise for what I said to him before I did. I caused a great deal of pain to many I loved and there's nothing I can do with my father to make it better. Nothing.'

'I know.' She'd done the same, but her mistake had revealed her family's true nature and the shallowness of their love for her. That had been a far more bitter pill to swallow than her exile from society. 'Your family loves you and they'll forgive you if you ask, but you have to forgive yourself first.'

Silas spun Mary around and she held on tight to him before easing her grip as they settled back into their steady pace. She was right, he needed to speak with his mother, but it was difficult, especially when every conversation they'd had in the last few days had been mere words from devolving into an argument. Years ago he hadn't been able to tell her what was in his heart. He wasn't sure how he could do it now, to stand before her and risk being vulnerable as he'd done with Mary and have her fail to understand him as she had before, but he couldn't leave England with this rift unhealed either. Once he settled the bank issue he'd speak with her and return to America without this guilt and heartache hanging over him. He wanted a relationship with his family, the kind Lottie described of holidays together and visits, not the distance and awkwardness that had marked the last eight years since he left for Liverpool. They'd been left to think he'd forgotten about them. He wanted his mother to know that he had never forgotten her or stopped loving or worrying about her.

The dance drew to a close and they stood still, their gazes locked as the last notes of the music drifted away. Silas studied Mary. In the face of her bravery in coming here tonight and facing all the busybodies standing on the edge of the dance floor he'd felt like a coward for keeping his truth from her. She hadn't derided him for what had happened, but maintained the faith in him that she'd shown since the ball in Baltimore. They might not have linked their lives together because of love, but it was there between them—perhaps it had been all along and it had taken coming to England and facing down both of their pasts to bring it out. Whatever it was, he wanted her to know that from this moment forward this was more than a partnership or business investment, but a true marriage.

'I love you, Mary.' He raised her hand to his lips and pressed a kiss to the satin-gloved back, the heat of her skin evident through the thin material.

'I love you, Silas.' She curled her fingers to hold on tight to his, each breath making her chest rise and fall with the anticipation and desire to truly be close to one another. The entire room fell away until it was simply the two of them, untouched by anything else except their love. Silas wanted to hold on to this moment for ever, the two of them out of reach of everyone and everything that threatened to intrude on their contentment, but the applause around them forced him to lower her hands, though he didn't release her. She was his and he would never let her go.

He escorted her off the dance floor to a quiet corner near the back of the room away from his family and anyone's intrusion.

'Why are you here with me instead of trying to win over the Marquess to come to America?' Mary teased, her breath warm against his cheek as he tilted down to hear her beautiful voice over the music of a rousing reel.

'All in good time.'

'Mary?' a female voice said over the dance music and Mary's giggles.

Mary's face went white as she peered over Silas's shoulder. He turned to see a woman with Mary's blonde hair and brown eyes standing behind them.

'J-Jane,' Mary stammered.

'I can't believe it's you.' Jane threw her arms around Mary and hugged her tightly. Mary slowly brought her hands up to grip her sister before throwing off all abandon and hugging her as tightly as Millie and Lottie had hugged Silas at his return. It heartened him to see the welcome and to know that at least one member of Mary's family hadn't shunned or forgotten her. Perhaps whatever peace Mary had promised Silas that he would find here, she might, through this reunion discover it, too.

The sisters held each other at arm's length, admiring the changes that had happened since they'd last seen one another, their excited words tripping over each other as they spoke before they settled enough to have a true conversation.

'Congratulations on your son,' Mary complimented, tears glistening in her eyes as she clutched her sister.

'He's the most beautiful little boy you've ever seen, although with his small belly and no hair, he looks more like Father than anyone else, but Mother says he has my eyes and Peter, well, you know our brother, he has little interest in children.' Jane laughed, unaware of the tightness in Mary's smile at the mention of the rest of her family. It wasn't intentional, Silas could tell, simply the failure to understand how much their lives had deviated since Mary had been gone.

'This is my husband, Silas Fairclough. He's Lady Falconmore's brother.'

'Why didn't you write to me that you were married and that you were in London?' Jane appeared crestfallen that her sister had not reached out to her while they were at last in the same city.

'I haven't had the chance. I've been in Baltimore for some time and it took a while for your letters to reach me. We left for England shortly after the service and we'll be here for a while before we return home.'

'We must find a way to meet again before you leave. You have to see your nephew. Oh, Mary, I've missed you so much.'

Mary clasped Jane tight as she hugged her again, unable to believe that after so much time they were really here together. She should have written to her, she should have given her the chance to be the sister she'd always been instead of fearing her husband and all the many horrors Mary had imagined, the ones that had yet to come true and might never come true. Despite the rest of her family, here was someone who did still love and care for her and

who would continue to defy everyone to keep
Mary in her life. She should have believed in
Jane's love for her the way she'd come to believe in Silas's and not allowed her worries to
keep them apart. 'We'll find a way to meet
again, I promise.'

'Yes, we will.'

'Jane, what the devil are you doing?' a man
who wasn't Silas thundered. Mary and Jane
stepped apart to see Jane's husband, Lord
Longford, bearing down on them. His face
was as red as the rose in his buttonhole as he
glared at his wife and Mary. Over his shoulder,
the rest of the women watched while pretending not to and Mary's stomach tightened. The
scene she'd feared playing out in the entrance
hall with Lord Falconmore was about to play
out here, much to everyone's delight.

'You remember my sister, Mary.' Jane's
shoulders drooped as she clasped her hands
together and stared at the floor, the fire of defi-
ance she'd shown in promising Mary that they
would meet again extinguished.

'Yes, I remember her,' Lord Longford
hissed, saving all his venom for Mary. 'How

dare you speak to my wife or show your face in good society?'

'I have every right to speak to Jane, as she does to me, and as much right to be at my sister-in-law's wedding ball as anyone,' Mary shot back. She would not give him or the people watching the satisfaction of seeing her crumble or slink away under his imperious sneer, the one filled with every accusation of harlot and fallen women that her father and brother had thrown at her. She was no longer the woman he was looking down his crooked nose at and she would never be that woman again.

Lord Longford recoiled at Mary's frank response, but it wasn't enough to make him abandon his effort to shame her. The man was persistent in his spite. 'I know Lord Falconmore made an imprudent match with that woman of questionable lineage, but I didn't think he was capable of stooping so low as to allow her disgraceful family to taint his home.'

'You know nothing of his life and family any more than you know about me or who I am. Therefore, I'll thank you to keep your opinions of all of us to yourself.'

'How dare you address me in such a manner, harlot?'

'Careful how you speak to Lady Mary,' Silas hissed, stepping between her and Lord Longford, matching him in height and stature. 'I won't shrink from calling out any man who insults my wife.'

'Do you know what kind of woman your wife is?'

Silas stepped closer, almost nose to nose with the Earl. 'Why don't you enlighten me and give me a reason to meet you at dawn?'

Lord Longford's confidence, the one fed by his belief that he had the right to sneer at Mary, faltered in the face of Silas's courage. Mary held her breath, afraid that Lord Longford might call out Silas or meet his warning with a punch or worse. The music of the reel grated on Mary's nerves while the two men faced each other, each waiting for the other to do something and decide the matter. The ballroom waited, too, a noticeable hush leaving only the music to fill the air.

'Is there a problem, gentleman?' Lord Falconmore appeared at Silas's side, studying the tense men. He was calm in the face of these two cocks facing each other, but there was no mistaking his strength as a marquess and the owner of this house.

'I won't have my wife tarnished by the likes of her,' Lord Longford snarled, levelling an accusing finger at Mary.

'Are you daring to address my sister-in-law in such coarse terms?' Lord Falconmore challenged and Lord Longford jerked down the edges of his waistcoat.

'No, milord, I'm simply careful about my wife's reputation.'

'Then perhaps you should go home where it cannot be sullied instead of lingering here. I'll be sure in the future to address your concerns by withholding any invitations, as well as my support in the House of Lords, so as not to offend your delicate sensibilities.'

'But, milord—' Lord Longford's face went white with his shock before Lord Falconmore cut him off.

'Good evening, Lord Longford. Don't let me keep you from your indignant exit.'

Lord Longford shrank back as if he'd smelled something foul, but he said no more. He reached around Silas and tugged Jane away from Mary. Jane didn't resist, but stood beside him as silent and shy as their mother had always been around their father. Mary longed to pull her back, to insist that she didn't have to go with this bully, but she did. He was her husband and she did not have the strength of character to stand up to him that the last four years had instilled in Mary.

Millie stepped up beside Mary, facing Lord Longford with the same determination as her husband. 'It's too bad you and Lady Longford have to leave so soon, for we were just about to discuss a shopping excursion. I was hoping Lady Mary and Lady Longford could join us, but I see that won't be the case.'

'No, it won't. Good evening, Lord Falconmore, Lady Falconmore,' Lord Longford mumbled before taking Jane by the arm and dragging her off into the crowd.

Mary wanted to follow after her sister, but she remained where she was, watching as Jane turned back to her, the anguish on her face at being ripped away from Mary for the second time echoing in Mary's heart. It was all too much like four years ago and she inwardly cried for what Jane would have to endure from her husband and eventually Mary's parents when Jane returned home and Lord Longford made the incident known. He was sure to be that petty.

'Thank you, Lord Falconmore, for your support,' Silas offered.

'It was my pleasure. If there's anything else I can do for you, please don't hesitate to let me know.'

'There is, but I fear tonight isn't the time to discuss it,' Silas said, trying to bring some lightness into the heavy mood surrounding them.

'Then the day after tomorrow. Pay me a visit and we'll chat while the ladies are off spending our money.'

'We'll have a grand time of it, too,' Millie promised. 'I'll take you to all the best modistes and haberdashers in London. Mary will look like a queen by the time I'm through with her.'

Mary did her best to smile and thank her sister-in-law, appreciating her kindness and the same optimism that she shared with Silas, but there were no dresses or bonnets that could take away the pain of losing Jane.

A footman approached the Marquess and

whispered in his ear. Lord Falconmore nodded, then faced Silas. 'It seems Lord Longford is refusing to go without making a scene
in the entrance hall. If you'll excuse me, I have
an earl who needs to once again be reminded
of his place.'

He strolled off with the footman, leaving
Mary and Silas alone, except they weren't
alone, surrounded by everyone who watched
and whispered about them. Millie glanced
across the ballroom to where Lottie stood with
Lilian, both of them wondering what had happened.

'I'd better tell Lottie and Mother about it before they hear something from someone else.'
Millie gave Mary's arm a reassuring squeeze.
'Stay as long as you like and let us know if
there is any more trouble.'

'Thank you.' Mary was grateful when
Millie walked off towards Lottie and Lilian.
Mary wanted to be far from the crowds and
the music and the too-bright chandeliers. She
didn't regret standing up to Lord Longford and
she was grateful for the Falconmores' support,
but the events of tonight were proving taxing.
However, she couldn't leave, not yet. If she and

Silas left, it would give her detractors the victory they craved.

'Let's dance,' Mary insisted.

Silas glanced at the people around them. 'Are you sure?'

'Yes.'

Silas gripped her hand and led her back out on to the floor where they took their places for the quadrille. She followed him through the dance, holding her head high, facing each new partner with a smile and self-assurance that she didn't always feel. If it weren't for Lord Falconmore, who'd returned to the ballroom to keep an eye on his guests, she was certain her partners would run away from her like rats off a sinking ship.

'I'm sorry, Mary,' Silas said as he led her through a turn. 'I didn't mean for tonight to go like this. I wanted them to see in you what I see.'

'They never will.'

Silas understood that now. He thought he was going to have to strike Lord Longford, but that wouldn't have changed anything, it simply would have added to the already sordid tale he'd caught snippets of as they'd walked to the ballroom. 'It was selfish of me to insist on your coming.'

She'd understood the situation better than he ever could and he had refused to listen, thinking his belief in her could overcome anything. This wasn't the husband he wanted to be, blind to what the person in front of him was trying to tell him, only able to see and hear what he wanted for them instead. It's how his parents had been with him and look where that had led him.

'It no longer matters. We won't have to see them again. This part of my life is over and it feels good to finally cast if off.'

'Do you mean that?' He hadn't expected this.

'I do. I came to England and this ball to look my past in the eye so it wouldn't ever trouble me ever again and I have. This was my life once, but not any more. My life is with you, in America, and I don't regret leaving this one behind.'

The dance ended, bringing them to a standstill in the middle of the other couples on the floor. He marvelled at the spirit she showed in the face of Lord Longford and Silas's mistakes. He thought the evening had turned into a disaster but he'd been wrong. Mary had faced her demons and conquered them the way he'd wanted her to, the way he longed to do with his own.

'Then let's go home.' There was nothing more for them to prove to anyone or even themselves by remaining here.

'Yes, let's.'

He offered Mary his arm and escorted her out of the room. Together they walked with their backs erect, their shoulders straight, ignoring the people who sneered at them when they passed. Those people and their opinions no longer mattered to them. Mary had faced her troubles and conquered them the way Silas would face his. He hadn't failed her as a husband, but stood beside her and helped her be strong. As they walked out of the Falconmore house and into the waiting carriage, the optimism that had made him a success filled him again.

Chapter Fifteen

'I'm sorry, Mr Fairclough, I'm afraid I can't grant you the patent,' Mr Williams announced from across his immaculately organised desk. It'd been three days since the ball and despite the dinner at Rules scheduled for tomorrow night, Mr Williams had requested this morning meeting with Silas. It wasn't like Silas to jump at a summons, but the moment he'd received Mr Williams's note he'd hailed a hack and hurried here as fast as he could. He'd suspected something less than palatable, but he hadn't expected this.

'If additional assurances are required from Jasper King or others, financial ones perhaps from my bank, I'm more than happy to provide those.' Silas wasn't going to take 'no' for an answer especially with something this important.

'Additional assurances or financial references aren't why I asked you to meet with me today, but something less tangible.' Mr Williams exchanged a worried look with Mr Cooper.

Mr Williams's inability to spit out the reason why he couldn't give Silas the patent frustrated Silas. He wanted the designer to say the words and stop fiddling around with his pens like a nervous old maid. Silas opened his mouth to tell him so and then shut it. He'd get nowhere by irritating Mr Williams with so frank an assessment of his negotiating skills. As long as Silas was in this office and they were sitting across from one another speaking like civilised gentlemen, there was still a chance that Silas could convince him to grant the patent. 'Explain your concerns, Mr Williams, and we'll deal with them. As I've discovered in my many years of business, there are very few obstacles that can't be overcome.'

'They aren't necessarily obstacles, Mr Fairclough, but grave concerns one of my investors has about doing business with you.'

'Then arrange a meeting and allow me to speak to the gentleman. I'm sure I can set his mind at ease.'

'I'm afraid that isn't possible.' Mr Williams fiddled with the pens, knocking one to the side before he stood it upright again. 'Most of my backers are titled men with more ambition and investment sense than your average aristocrat, but many of their old prejudices about sullying their hands with business, among other things, still remain.'

Silas's stomach began to sink. He'd been broadsided by Mr Williams's refusal of the patent, but he could see his reason behind it coming as clearly as a locomotive roaring down a track. He inwardly shuddered to think of the consequences for him, and Mary. The ball the other night had left them believing the past was dead. Mr Williams was about to prove that it wasn't. 'What objections could they possibly have to making additional money from their investments, money that will add to the grandeur of their titles?'

'One of my most important backers is a good friend of Lord Longford's. I'm not at liberty to say who he is, but he has supplied a great deal of the capital that has allowed me to take my ideas from mere drawings to working locomotives. It's because of him and the large amount of money he's invested in my enterprise that I have to refuse the patent.'

'What objection could he possibly have to being involved in this particular venture, especially one that won't even be in England where it can trouble him?' He knew exactly what this friend of Lord Longford's objections were, but if Mr Williams was going to allow his dreams to be controlled by this narrow-minded backer and turn down a profitable opportunity because of some lords' overabundance of concern for social gossip then Silas wanted Mr Williams to say it aloud.

'My backer does not have objections to the money or opportunities your business plan entails, but to the reputation it and those connected to you might bring to bear on him.' Mr Williams tugged at his collar, hoping that this was enough for Silas to understand. It was, but he wasn't going to let him get away without saying it outright.

'The reputation of which people, Mr Williams?' Silas perched on the edge of his chair and rested his elbow on the desk, fighting the urge to sweep everything off the top of it, including the pens Mr Williams kept playing with.

Mr Cooper continued to hunch over his paperwork, pretending not to listen.

Mr Williams let go of the pens and sat back in his chair to place some distance between him and Silas. 'Your wife's reputation, Mr Fairclough.'

Silas trilled his fingers on the wood, working hard to control his temper. 'Are you besmirching my wife's good name based on rumours you've heard from *illustrious* men, the kind that will give you money, but never allow a man of your common background to dine at their table? Are those the people making decisions about your company and its future?'

'I have no choice. If it was up to me I'd offer you the patent, but without this man's investments I can't continue my work. My company would fold and I'd lose everything. Surely you must understand that?'

Silas stood, making Mr Williams press back even further in his chair. 'I do, but what I don't understand is your cowardice. A man of your genius should tell him to take his pounds and prudery elsewhere. If he refuses to make money and build a future because of some objection to a lady to whom he has no connection, who no longer resides in this country, and you allow him to have a say in the running of your company, then you and your enterprise are going to fail. Not today, but tomorrow when every opportunity has passed you by because some toffee-nosed lord who never worked a day in his life told you what to do.'

Silas strode out of the office, not bothering to close the door behind him or acknowledge the two clerks he passed who stopped writing to look up at him. They'd overheard his conversation and the rare moment of emotion when he'd been unable to check himself. Good, let them hear that their employer was a coward, let those among them who were using their position as a stepping stone or a chance to make money while pursuing their own ventures take this lesson to heart. A timid man who bound himself to the will of others did not succeed.

Silas walked away from Mr Williams's office, disappointment nipping at him. It wasn't only Richard and the Baltimore Southern he'd failed in not securing the patent, but Mary. For the second time in as many days the promise he'd made to her that her past didn't matter had been proven wrong. It had risen up as she'd feared to bite them both and there was nothing he could do to overcome it, to make Mr Williams see the foolishness of his decision or to convince his investor to crack open his stubbornly shut mind. Without the patent Silas would have to find another engine and attempt to acquire it, assuming some lord with a prissy sense of things didn't control that engineer, too. It might take months in England to discover a new one, leaving the Baltimore Southern's new rail lines fallow and Richard with the burden of managing things. It might weaken him enough to deliver the fatal blow, his death hastened by Silas's failure. He couldn't have that, nor could he go home and tell Mary the real reason why they must extend their stay. If there was an American option he would seize it, but there wasn't. People's inability to think ahead and build foundries for rails extended to steam engines, too. They thought they could rely on England and her goods for ever, but Silas knew better. Perhaps he could convince a designer to follow him across the Atlantic, but this would also take time and an honest explanation for Mary, one he was loath to give.

Silas slowed his steps. Not since the two

years after his father's illness when he'd risen each morning to work at the Foundation, all the while longing to be elsewhere, had Silas felt so trapped by a situation. He wanted to return to his mother's house, order their things packed, board the next steamer to Baltimore and leave this frustration behind, but he couldn't. Lottie and Millie, despite their disappointment, might understand his abrupt departure, but his mother wouldn't and all chance for a reconciliation with her would be lost. He'd been so preoccupied with business that he hadn't spoken to his mother as Mary had urged. His leaving might make it so that they never discussed what had happened and it continued to hang over them, but he couldn't stay here. He refused to allow Mary to take the blame for losing the engine patent. It would undo everything she'd accomplished by attending the ball.

He hailed a hack and gave the driver instruction to take him to his solicitor. He would finish arranging the new trust for his mother and, if he could, discover who had stolen the bank notes. It would all be concluded as quickly as possible so he and Mary could return to Baltimore. He wished he could do it before he had to tell Mary the truth about Mr Williams. He could lie to her, but she would see through it. He wanted no deception between them, but he didn't want to hurt her or ruin everything that she'd accomplished when she'd faced Lord Longford either. With luck, it wouldn't come to that, but as he'd seen this morning, his luck had become precarious.

'Leave London, so soon?' Mary gasped when Silas told her.

'Our life is in America, not here. I see no reason to linger somewhere that has caused us so much misery.' Silas paced back and forth across his small bedroom like a tiger in a cage.

'It hasn't all been misery. I've enjoyed working with the women, and getting to know your family. I'd like us to spend more time with Lottie and Millie, and to thank Millie and her husband for what they did for me at the ball.'

Her hesitation about going home surprised him. He thought she'd want to leave on the success of the ball. Silas straightened his cufflinks, unable to tell her how far the incident at the ball had crept into their lives and was now affecting the future. 'I'm sorry. I'd like for us to stay longer, but we can't. There's business that must be seen to in America and I fear for Richard's health if we dally here too long.'

'Did you receive a letter from him? Is something wrong?'

'No, but like you I'm concerned about him and his future, and ours.' He leaned hard on the fireplace mantel, watching the small fire in it flicker and threaten to go out. The chill in the room was as pervasive as his shame. He should tell her the truth, but couldn't risk hurting her like that.

'You didn't receive the patent. That's why Mr Williams asked you to see him today, isn't it?' She'd guessed the truth as easily as his mother used to do.

'I was unable to convince Mr Williams, or I should say his investor, of the validity of my proposal and it was clear that there was nothing I could say to change either men's minds.'

'And you're giving up, just like that. Why?'

'You're right, Mary, not every obstacle can be overcome.'

'This isn't the Silas I know. Something else happened. What was it? Tell me so I can help you.' She rested a hand on his shoulder. Her touch should have soothed him, but it increased the conflict between being honest with her and protecting her. He avoided her gaze, afraid she would see the truth in his eyes. She didn't need to see his face to guess. 'It was because of me and my past, wasn't it?'

'No.'

'You're a terrible liar, Silas.'

'So what if I am? I failed to receive the patent, not because of something you did, but because of small-minded men, the kind that infest London's upper classes making it difficult for men of real dreams and visions who weren't born on the right side of the Thames to achieve them.'

'Small-minded men who never would have had a reason to look down on you and your ideas if it hadn't been for me. How many patrons will your mother lose because of it, how much more damage will my being here do to the young women she helps?'

'None, because I set up the trust today. Nothing and no one can come between my mother and the safety of her living ever again.'

'But what about the Foundation? She needs patrons and she's a proud woman who sees securing them as part of her work. Charity from you will rob her of that.'

'Lord Falconmore's influence will guarantee supporters.'

'But what about the missing bank drafts? We can't leave until you've figured out what happened to them and your letters. Whoever stole the money might do it again.'

'My mother is right. The Foundation business is not mine to interfere in. I gave up that right when I left five years ago.'

'And you wish to do it again?'

'I'm not sneaking away, but leaving somewhere that has nothing for me or us. I despise London and the way it's tried to beat us down despite everything we've accomplished.'

'What about your family? Will you leave them behind again to wonder what happened to you and why you left?'

'Mother will probably be glad I'm gone instead of here prying into her business. I'm nothing but a disappointment to her.'

'You aren't. They don't care about what happened before, only that you're here and with them, opening up the possibility that you'll be a part of their lives again. You can't take that away from them or us.'

Silas slid his father's signet ring on and off his finger. Everything that had happened today and all Mary said was tumbling through his mind until he couldn't keep anything straight. She was asking him to stay in the face of his desire to leave, to remain in this confusion when all he wanted was to flee from it. He looked about the room, the old feeling of being stifled and confined sweeping over him. 'I have to go out.'

'Where?'

He took up his walking stick and hat. 'Some place where I can think.'

'I'll come with you.'

'No, I need to be alone.'

'Silas, please.'

'I said I need to be alone.'

Mary watched as he flung his redingote over his shoulders and stepped out into the hall, leaving her the way Preston had done.

No, he's nothing like Preston. He's had a shock and he needs some time to think about it. Then he'll be back. He'll devise some solution, a way out of this tangle. He always does.

She said this over and over, struggling to believe it. His marriage to her had cost him the much-needed patent. He might deny that fact it in front of her, but surely he thought it even now as she heard the front door open and close. He wasn't going off to think about the patent or whether or not they should leave, but whether or not he should return to her. She thought she'd triumphed over her past when she'd stood up to Lord Longford, but she hadn't and it had cost Silas what he'd wanted the most.

Mary pressed her hand to her chest, her stays tight beneath her dress.

I never should have come back to England.

She should go downstairs to the Foundation and help the women instead of sitting here fretting about what might happen, but she couldn't. She couldn't cross into the building and face those women who looked up to her. She was a fraud unworthy of their respect and that of her husband's.

Mary began to pace, afraid of what might happen if she and Silas returned to America in haste. He might set her aside to find a wife who could bring him more honour and grandeur than anything that she could bestow on him by her faint connection with her family and she would be left with nothing. The divorce laws in America would make this easier for him to do and then she would be as shamed there as she was here, cast off by one man to sink into the obscurity from which he'd plucked her.

Unless there's a child.

She laid her hands over her flat stomach. Her courses still hadn't come, making this possibility more and more likely as the days passed. Silas believed in doing right by those he loved, but to keep him only because of a child brought her no comfort. A marriage of duty and obligation wasn't what she wanted, not after the love they'd shared over the last few weeks, the one that had given Mary hope that her married life would be different and happier than her parents'. She'd never witnessed true affection between them, instead she'd seen how alone and isolated her mother had grown through the years. She'd had children, but because of her position she'd only enjoyed the most tenuous of connections with them. It had made it even easier for her to turn her back on Mary when the time had come.

Mary rose and searched the room for a calendar, but there was none. There was one on the desk in the sitting room and without thinking she made her way downstairs to furiously flip through it and count the days since her last courses. She checked and rechecked the dates, but the travel and everything that had happened with Richard made her unsure of when her courses had last been. It must have been before the wedding in Baltimore for they had not happened on the steam ship or during their time in London. She could not say for certain that she was with child, but the likelihood it was possible was growing stronger with each passing day.

Mary swallowed hard against the lump in her throat, remembering the start of the blood the last time and how it had ended with all her hopes for redemption. It could happen again, one miscarriage might mean others and Silas would have even more grounds to leave her. What would she do without him? Grow alone in Richard's house in Baltimore, shunned and forgotten.

'Mary, are you well?' Lilian approached her in the low light of the room.

Mary couldn't hide the tears from her this time, but shook her head, sinking down on to the couch and sobbing. Lilian sat beside her and held her until the tears subsided and the words began. She told her everything: what had happened with Preston, at the ball and her time with Silas. Lilian listened, not blaming her or shying away from the truth, but embracing Mary and taking in everything she told her.

'I love him and I'm afraid he'll come to resent and hate me because of my past,' Mary choked out, wiping her eyes with the back of her hand. 'I have already cost him the patent and who knows what else.'

'Silas isn't like that.'

'I know, but it's so hard not to be afraid.'

'I understand.' Lilian rested her hands in her lap, studying her long fingers and the gold wedding band that still adorned her left hand. 'When Silas sailed off, I thought it was because of all of the demands I'd placed on him after his father died. I was so focused on keeping the Foundation going, to honour my husband's memory and to bury my grief, that I couldn't see the truth of what was before me. I refused to see how much he needed to follow his heart the way his father had. I didn't understand his need to pursue his dreams or support him the way you do, and I drove him away. I've been careful with him since his return, afraid I might do it again.'

'He wants to be here with you, but he thinks you don't approve of what he does.' Mary hated to see Lilian suffer the same torment that racked Mary and Silas. 'He regrets what he did with you and his father.'

'And I regret how I treated him. I approve of anything and anyone that makes him happy and the railroad and you make him very happy.' Lilian took Mary's hands, a determination in her eyes that reminded Mary of how Silas looked whenever he talked of his plans and his belief that he would achieve them. 'I've watched the two of you together. Silas's face lights up when you're beside him as much as it does when he discusses his railroad. You understand him in a way neither I nor his father ever could and you encourage him in his ventures as a wife should, as I used to do when I worked beside my husband. I know the value in that because it's the thing someone like Silas needs the most when a dream is on the verge of failing or he's facing tough times with no signs of a remedy. He won't leave you, Mary, but he needs you very much. Don't be afraid to go to him, to speak to him the way I've been afraid to do. Don't let this distance grow between you like the one between me and Silas. Be brave and honest with him and you'll see that everything will be all right.'

Mary stared down at her wedding ring, the symbol of the vows connecting her to Silas. Lilian was right. In the circle of his arms the distance from her family didn't feel as all consuming and the loneliness it had created in her life faded away. She didn't want to lose that comfort or his love because of her fears. Silas was facing a bitter disappointment and she refused to allow him to do it alone. She would support him and help him remember that he was the success he believed and that there was a solution to these troubles like there were to all his others. She would be beside him to help him find it.

Chapter Sixteen

Silas leaned against the wrought-iron railing to watch the trains pass by on the tracks below, the sound of the pistons as they turned the wheels, the smell of soot and steam failing to calm him. The truth was, it never had. In all the times he'd come here as a young man to try to find answers or think things through, there had never been a solution in the engines, simply the space to try to find one. The same held true today. His dreams had started here and he was afraid they might die here, too. He'd placed a great deal of the future on securing the English patent. He wasn't sure what he would do without it. He would have to think of something else, some new plan, but at the moment, with the memory of Mary's anguish haunting him along with every failure that had marked him when he'd lived in London and when he'd left it, he could think of nothing and it scared him.

'Silas?'

Silas turned to see Mary approaching, her yellow-cotton gown bright against the overcast day. He wanted to rush to her and take her in his arms, but he didn't move, ashamed of himself and the way he'd stormed away from her. This wasn't the man he was, but it was the one being in England made him and he hated it. 'How did you know where to find me?'

'Where else would you be?'

She was right, just as she'd been right all along about her past and the impact it would have on them. He'd been naive to dismiss her just as he'd been blind to think he could succeed in London. There had never been success for him here like there had been in America, not in business or among those he loved. 'I shouldn't have walked away from you. I'm sorry, it was wrong of me.'

'We are all allowed to be wrong from time to time.'

'I was wrong about a lot of things. I failed you, Mary, I failed us both.'

'No, you didn't. You built me up and made me believe in myself when I wanted to fade into the woodwork, you helped me see that I'm more than my mistakes.'

'I made you promises that I couldn't keep.'

'Not because you didn't believe in them, but because others are too petty and shallow to see who I am the way you do, the way I sometimes fail to do. Let them have their prejudices and gossip, it doesn't matter to us.'

'Not this time. I needed that patent.'

'And you'll think of some way around it, another way to get what you want. You don't give up that easily, Silas. I wouldn't be married to you if you did.'

Her faith in him offered more comfort and peace than the passing trains or even leaving England ever could. With her beside him, he felt like the man he was in America who didn't allow anything to stop him, who had made a success of himself by believing in the possibility of his dreams and those of the people he cared about. He wasn't a failure or a man to allow setback to stop him, but a success who would carry on as he had before but with Mary by his side. 'Then you're ready to go home?'

'You can't leave yet, Silas.' His mother's voice carried beneath the distant howl of a train whistle.

Silas stood, amazed to see her here, too. She wore the thick burgundy pelisse he'd sent her for Christmas a few years ago. She slowly approached him and the memory of that early morning ten years ago outside his father's room echoed between them. Then Mary's hand on his arm dispelled the pain and uncertainty of that awful day and the hesitation marking this one.

'Ever since you were a little boy I knew you weren't like Millie or Lottie or even your father,' his mother said, coming to stand in front of him. 'You care a great deal about those you love and the women that we've helped through the years, but it was obvious that this wasn't the life for you.'

'Then why did you and Father try to foist it on me?'

'Because like you, your father loved what he did and he knew it would be far more difficult for his daughters to inherit the Foundation and keep it running than it would be for a son. With a man at the helm after his passing he felt certain that everything we'd accomplished would continue. He didn't mean to dismiss your dreams, but he was perhaps too focused on his own to realise the pressure he'd placed on you, the way I did after he passed, but know this, Silas—he loved you and wanted you to grow up to be a forthright man and you have. He would be very proud to see you now.'

Silas drank in the words he'd longed to hear ever since the night his father had passed, but another care still weighted on him. 'And you?'

'I wanted you here because I love you and I wrongly believed that through you a part of your father could still be involved in his dream, but you aren't your father and his dreams aren't yours, and there is nothing wrong with that, nothing at fault and no one to blame. You are your own man, exactly how it should be, and I'm proud of you and everything you've done.' She hugged him close and he held her, the noise of the train and London fading away until his mother stepped back, a wry smile decorating her lips. 'Even when you sneak around the Foundation in the middle of the night to look through the ledgers.'

'You knew about that?'

'There isn't much that happens at the Foundation that I don't know about. I only wish I'd allowed you to look at the ledgers instead of stopping you from doing all you could to make sure we were taken care of, the way you always have. Starting today, the books are yours to examine. I want to put the issue of the bank drafts and everything else behind us for good.'

'So do I.'

'Then let's go home. We still have a great deal of work to do.' She linked her arm in Silas's and the three of them made their way out of the train station towards home.

'Mr Fairclough,' Tibbs greeted when they arrived at the Fairclough house. 'There's a Mr Perkins and his clerk to see you in the sitting room.'

'Who are they?' Mary asked as she and Lilian removed their coats and handed them to the valet.

'The bank manager and the one man who can give us some clue to the identity of the person who stole my money.' Silas handed his coat to Tibbs, then whispered to him, 'Send for the constable, I want him to take a full report of the clerk's description of the thief.'

'Yes, sir.'

Silas entered the sitting room where the bank manager and his reedy clerk waited.

'Mr Fairclough, this is Mr Jones. He was the man who regularly cashed the bank drafts for Mr Smith. Mr Jones, tell Mr Fairclough what the gentleman who made the transactions looks like.'

'Yes, sir, he came in once a month, he was of a medium build with a dapper way about him, dressing fine, but not too fine.'

'Why did you allow him to cash the bank drafts?'

'His papers were in order and I wasn't from Mr Perkins's bank, but the one they acquired. I wasn't aware of the standing order of the double letters. If I'd known, I wouldn't have allowed him to cash the drafts.'

'Was there anything physically remarkable about him?' Silas asked as the manager squirmed at realising how much he and his institution were responsible for the mishap. Let the man worry, it would encourage him to help more than he already was. 'Were there any other distinguishing traits that can help us identify him?'

The clerk scratched his smooth chin, looking up at the ceiling a moment before he answered, 'He had strange eyes, not quite the same colour.'

Silas and his mother exchanged stunned looks. There was one man they knew who matched that description and, as if hearing himself spoken of, he appeared at that moment, ledger in hand.

'Mrs Fairclough, I wish to speak to you about settling the butcher's account.' Mr Edwards looked up from his ledger, dropping it on the floor in surprise at seeing Mr Jones in the sitting room.

'That's him.' Mr Jones levelled a finger at Mr Edwards. 'That's Mr Smith, the man who signed for the bank drafts.'

Mr Edwards glanced about at the assembled people. Silas waited for him to defend himself or dispute the charge, to sputter out a string of excuse for what had happened. He did neither, but sprinted for the door. Silas was on him in a flash, tripping him in the entryway and pinning his arm behind his back so he couldn't move.

The front door swung open and Tibbs entered with the constable.

'What's all this, then?' the officer demanded, seeing Silas holding a fighting Mr Edwards against the floorboards.

'I wish to press charges against this man for theft,' Silas demanded, hauling Mr Edwards to his feet. In quick sentences he told the constable the story of the missing drafts and letters before Mr Jones and the bank manager offered their evidence.

'After everything my mother did for you, how could you betray her like that?' Silas demanded as the constable held a chastened Mr Edwards by the arm.

'I wanted to get away, to get out of London. I've spent years in this stinking pit, scratching out a living, forced to keep books for other people like my last employer, who had no compunction about letting me sink because he frittered away his money on cards and women, leaving me with nothing, no future, no money, no reference, nothing. I wanted the country and the peace it offered.'

'And you thought to get it by stealing my

money and placing my mother and sisters and the women here at risk.'

'They were never in real danger. I stopped your sisters' letters from being posted while they lived here and burned yours after I took the bank drafts out. Once I was in the country, which I would have been if you hadn't returned, your correspondence would have resumed.'

'Not before my mother and the women here lost everything.'

'You have enough money to save them, you always have. You don't know what it's like to be on the verge of failing completely, to not have enough to fill your stomach or sleep soundly at night.'

Silas stepped toe to toe with the unrepentant manager. 'I know more about that than you will ever realise. Unlike you, I pulled myself out of that horrid situation by sheer will. I didn't attempt to steal my way out of it. Where's the money you took? I want it back.'

'It's in Tom Smith's account,' Mr Jones said. 'He always deposited it there, saying it was for the Foundation.'

'We'll make sure it's returned to you at once, Mr Fairclough,' the bank manager promised.

'Come along then,' the constable said, dragging Mr Edwards out of the house.

The bank manager and his clerk left amid a torrent of apologies and assurance of the stability of the bank, none of which could assure Silas that his accounts and business would be safe with them.

By the time the sun began to set, Silas, Lilian and Mary were alone again in the sitting room, their tea growing cold on the table before them as they took in everything that had happened.

'Septimus will be heartbroken when he hears of this,' Lilian lamented. 'He recommended Mr Edwards, but the man had us all fooled. Except you, Silas. You suspected him from the beginning. I should have listened to you.'

'I had no proof, only the knowledge that he was closest to the drafts. I easily could have been mistaken. You gave him a second chance he didn't deserve and he took advantage of your kindness to help himself. I'll do everything I can to find a new manager before we return to Baltimore.'

Lilian rose, placed a kiss on Silas's cheek and looked lovingly on him. 'Thank you for all your help and everything you do for us, everything you've always done.'

'You know you can always count on me.'

She patted his hand where she held it between hers. 'I know.'

Lilian took her leave of Silas and Mary, the day as wearing on her as it was on them, but neither Mary nor Silas were ready to retire yet.

'Thank you for bringing my mother to the station. It means the world to me to have heard what she said about her and my father.' Silas pulled Mary close to him on the sofa, warming her against the chill of the encroaching evening. 'Never in all my life could I have imagined coming to London and finding peace, but I have, thanks to you.'

'And I you. I was afraid that everything here would take away what I've found with you, but it hasn't.'

'It never will. I love you, Mary, and I couldn't imagine a life without you.'

She took his hand and led him upstairs to their room. He followed her through the dark house. When the door was closed he embraced her, savouring the sweet smell of her and the heat of her body against his. She remained close to him, the quiet between them like a comforting blanket before she spoke. 'Watching you with your mother made me think that everything isn't lost with my family, that there must be some way to see Jane and all I have to do is find it.'

'Do you think it's possible?'

She wrapped her arms around his waist and looked up at him with a love to take his breath away. 'With you beside me, I think anything is possible.'

Chapter Seventeen

'Mr Fairclough, there's a young gentleman here to see you,' Tibbs announced as Mary and Silas sat in the dining room enjoying their breakfast.

'Who is it?' Silas asked. He'd been visiting a number of engineers over the last two weeks to review their work and find another engine, but he had no appointments with any of them today.

'He said he's an assistant of Mr Williams and would like to speak with you concerning the matter of locomotive engines.'

Silas and Mary exchanged hopeful glances.

'Maybe Mr Williams finally grew a backbone and stood up to his investors,' Silas mused. 'Send the gentleman in at once.'

Tibbs left and a moment later returned with

the young man who'd sat silently in Mr Williams's office during Silas's meetings with the engineer. He was dressed now as he had been before in a simple but well-cut suit that spoke of limited means, but a great deal of ambition, the way Silas had dressed in his early years in America. 'Mr Cooper, sir.'

Silas rose and waved the man towards an empty seat on the far side of table. 'Please, join us.'

Mr Cooper sat down, setting the rolled-up paper he carried under his left arm on the floor beside him. He made no move for the food.

'Would you like some breakfast?' Mary asked, pinning him with the same charming smile that she'd used to help win over the Baltimore investors what seemed like a lifetime ago.

'No, ma'am, thank you.'

'How can I help you?' Silas tried to put the man at ease, wondering what it was he'd come all the way here to tell him.

'As you know, Mr Fairclough, I was present during your initial conversation with Mr Williams involving the train-engine patent and again when he rejected your offer. I greatly apologise for his short-sightedness in denying you the patent. He's a brilliant engineer, but a timid man more suited to his drafting board than the head of a corporation.'

'Did Mr Williams send you here to apologise on his behalf?'

'No, I'm here on similar but different business. You see, Mr Fairclough, I'm not simply Mr Williams's clerk, but an engineer in my own right. I've been working with him these last few years to gain practical experience and knowledge and further develop my skills. However, due to Mr Williams and his investor's tight control over their work, I've had very few opportunities to present mine.' He lifted the roll of paper off the floor and held it up. 'May I show you this?'

Silas and Mary moved the dishes on the table out of the way to allow Mr Cooper to unroll the paper to reveal the plans for a new steam locomotive. It was like nothing Silas had ever seen before. It was different and more advanced than even Mr Williams's design.

'This is my idea for a new type of engine. I've developed a special valve gear that can be opened and closed with a bar that requires fewer men to operate and gives the engineer greater control over the flow of steam. This allows the engine to support more weight and increases the freight hauling power, and for the speed to be better adjusted once the engine is in motion.'

Silas studied the plans, marvelling at the genius of the design. It was exactly the kind of engine he'd hoped to win the American patent for, but this one was larger and more advanced and would do twice as much as the engine Silas had originally sought, assuming it really was Mr Cooper's idea.

'You didn't steal this from Mr Williams, did you?' Silas demanded, unwilling to gain an advantage by such underhanded means. His father had raised him with more ethics than that.

'No, Mr Fairclough, these designs and others I've been working on are entirely my own. I've never had the chance to test the designs and make any necessary refinements. Mr Williams is afraid not only of competition from others companies, but from men in his employ. It's why I've come to you. I want the chance to show the world my work and my talents.'

Silas exchanged a knowing look with Mary. 'That's certainly something I can sympathise with.'

'I believe that this is the locomotive you're searching for to help propel the Baltimore Southern's ambitions and that it will serve you better than any of Mr Williams's designs, which an engine like this could easily make obsolete.'

Mary studied the drawings, but Silas could tell by the small crease of confusion between her brows that they meant very little to her. They meant a great deal to him, however. He could see the brilliance of Mr Cooper's designs, where they had picked up on the flaws of previous engines including Mr Williams's, and improved upon them.

'This is excellent work,' Silas complimented. 'Where did you train?'

'I have no formal training, I learned through books and watching other mechanics and engineers over the years. As a result, few people are willing to take me seriously, but I believe that you will. You have the vision that Mr Williams and so many others lack. I'd like very much to come with you to America and work for the Baltimore Southern and give you access to this plan and many others that I have in mind. All I ask is for the chance to prove to you and everyone that I'm a real and true engineer.'

The man spoke with the same passion for experience that Silas had expressed with Richard all those years ago, reminding him of himself when he'd landed in Baltimore. He would give him that chance the same way Richard had given Silas his. 'Tell me more about your ideas.'

Silas and Mr Cooper discussed the plans and others he had for different mechanical components for well over an hour. Mary stayed with the gentlemen, playing the hostess and offering the young man tea and finally convincing him to accept food. When everything had been discussed and all the arrangements for Mr Cooper to join the railroad agreed upon, Silas stood and vigorously shook the young engineer's hand. 'Welcome to the Baltimore Southern Railway, Mr Cooper. I'll purchase your Cunard steamer ticket to America and write the necessary introduction letter for you to my manager and my business partner, Mr Richard Jackson.'

'Thank you, Mr Fairclough. You won't regret it.'

'No, I won't.'

Once Tibbs had shown Mr Cooper out, Mary came around the table, taking Silas in her arms and looking up at him with an adoration that was worth more than a thousand steam-engine plans. 'I told you you'd find a new way.'

'I can't take credit for this one, it fell in my lap.'

'But you have the vision to recognise his ideas and to act on them after people like Mr Williams didn't.'

'True, like I had the vision to make you my wife before some other Baltimore businessman snapped you up.'

'And when will we follow Mr Cooper to Baltimore? I have a bachelor's house there waiting for a woman's touch, a wedding ball to arrange and a nursery to decorate.'

Silas jerked back, studying Mary to see if she had told him what he thought she had just told him. 'Is it true?'

'It is.'

He picked her up and whirled her around with a hoot before setting her on her feet as if she were a fragile porcelain statue. 'You don't know how happy this makes me.'

'Me, too. Perhaps our child will have a marquess as a godfather?' she said with as much self-satisfied plotting as he regularly employed. 'You could ask him to do so when you suggest he come to America to see the railroad.'

'All in good time. We're here and I'm not ready to think about leaving my family or to miss the opportunity to see what other innovations and possibilities London has to offer, and I don't think you are either.'

'No, I'm not.' She rose up on her toes, touching her forehead to his, her breath teasing him with the chance to be in her arms as completely as a man and wife could be. 'I love you, Silas.'

'I love you, Mary.' He pressed his lips to hers, sealing his promise to her and himself that they would have a grand future. They would be together for always, standing beside each other through every joy and challenge life lobbed at them.

* * * * *

MILLS & BOON

Coming next month

AN UNCONVENTIONAL COUNTESS
Jenni Fletcher

'It's strange, but you might be the only person in the world who *can* understand.'

Anna felt her pulse quicken at the words. It was the same thing she'd thought when she'd told Samuel how she felt trapped, as if they truly *could* understand each other. As if maybe, despite everything, they might be a good match after all, just as the Baroness had said. The way he was looking at her now suggested he thought so, too, but how could that be possible? She was a shopkeeper and he was an earl...*maybe*. Or maybe not. There was an equal chance that he might remain a captain.

'I do understand.' She tried to keep her voice normal. 'Only my mother told me recently that bitterness and resentment weren't very attractive qualities. Shall I repeat her lecture?'

'Did it make you feel any better?'

'No, but it did make me think. Now I want to let go of the past and move on, wherever it leads me.'

'Wherever...?' He echoed the word as he lifted a hand to the side of her face, his fingers sliding gently across the curve of her cheek and beneath her chin, tilting it upwards. The touch sent a thrill of heat coursing through her body, making her feel as if every inch of

her skin was blushing. Thank goodness they were outside in the dark. Although they really shouldn't be. Not together and certainly not touching like this. No matter what he said about understanding each other, there were still too many obstacles between them. Only it was becoming hard to hold on to that thought.

'We ought to go in.' She swallowed nervously. 'You said it was time for supper.'

'Did I?' He moved closer, his jacket brushing against the front of her dress. 'I can't remember.'

'Yes. I don't think…'

Her words faltered as his arms closed around her waist, enveloping her in a feeling of strong masculine warmth. She didn't move or resist, too surprised to do anything as he leaned in towards her, his mouth moving slowly towards and then hovering above hers, so tanta-lisingly close that it was hard to believe they weren't already touching. She could feel the warmth of his breath as it skimmed across her cheek…and then there was a sensation of cold air as he moved to one side, gently grazing the edge of her mouth.

Continue reading
AN UNCONVENTIONAL COUNTESS
Jenni Fletcher

Available next month
www.millsandboon.co.uk

COMING SOON!

We really hope you enjoyed reading this book. If you're looking for more romance, be sure to head to the shops when new books are available on

Thursday 23rd January

To see which titles are coming soon, please visit

millsandboon.co.uk/nextmonth

MILLS & BOON